CW00448682

About the Author

John Virgo Brown was born in west London in 1951. He completed his education at the University of Surrey, graduating with a degree in microbiology in 1973, and spent his working life in the food and dairy industries. He retired in 2013, and in a futile attempt to avoid getting under his wife's feet, took a course in creative writing. This is his first novel.

To Francis & Dave

Joe

x

The Time Travelling Mushroom

John Virgo Brown

The Time Travelling Mushroom

Olympia Publishers
London

www.olympiapublishers.com
OLYMPIA PAPERBACK EDITION

Copyright © John Virgo Brown 2022

The right of John Virgo Brown to be identified as author of
this work has been asserted in accordance with sections 77 and 78
of the Copyright, Designs and Patents Act 1988.

All Rights Reserved

No reproduction, copy or transmission of this publication
may be made without written permission.
No paragraph of this publication may be reproduced,
copied or transmitted save with the written permission of the
publisher, or in accordance with the provisions
of the Copyright Act 1956 (as amended).

Any person who commits any unauthorised act in relation to
this publication may be liable to criminal
prosecution and civil claims for damage.

A CIP catalogue record for this title is
available from the British Library.

ISBN: 978-1-80074-166-9

This is a work of fiction.
Names, characters, places and incidents originate from the writer's
imagination. Any resemblance to actual persons, living or dead, is
purely coincidental.

First Published in 2022

Olympia Publishers
Tallis House
2 Tallis Street
London
EC4Y 0AB

Printed in Great Britain

Dedication

For Hazel, Sebbie and Leo.

The Time Travelling Mushroom

Prologue
Sussex, 14th October, 1066

"Bugger me, Bob," said William. "That was close!"

"Certainly was. Half our blokes thought it was game over when the English broke up our last bash at their shield wall, and legged it back to the boats."

"Don't blame them. I was nearly off myself!"

The two men surveyed the scene of carnage littering the softly rolling Sussex countryside to their front.

"Anyone we know out there?" asked Robert de Beaumont.

"Eustace caught an axe in his bollocks at the last minute. Beautiful up and under. I went over and congratulated the bloke who did it," replied William.

"Will he live, do you think?"

"He'll be OK. But there'll be no little Counts of Dieppe. Not official ones, anyway."

"What about the troops? Many gone?"

"Oh, few hundred, couple of thousand. Plenty more where they came from."

There was a pause in the conversation. Then William said, "You know what turned it?"

"It was that funny baldy bloke," Robert replied. "Their lines were rock solid till he came galloping out of them. Then half the English army set off after him. Our archers turned round to watch the fun and, bugger me, if they didn't join in and try and shoot him too. One of the arrows went too high and clocked poor old Harold in the eye. While they were distracted with that it gave us our chance to take them in the flank, and that was that. England 1 France 2."

"Strange bloke," mused William. "Funny clothes. He had sort of dark flappy tubes on his legs and a white shirt with something tied round his neck. Where do you think he was from?"

"Dunno," said Robert. "Wales?"

"What makes you say that, Bob?"

"My dad went there once. They wear funny clothes 'cos it's always pissing down with rain. Miserable buggers he said they were."

"We'll have to watch out for them, then. What do they call this place?"

"I don't think they call it anything. Hastings is a few miles away."

"We'll have to call it something," said William. "Every battle's got a name. We can't call it The Battle of nr. Hastings."

"How about Battle?"

"That would be really silly. That would make it The Battle of Battle."

"Sod it, why don't you just call it The Battle of Hastings? Nobody's going to be bothered *exactly* where it was."

"Battle of Hastings it is, then. What about me? What shall we call me?"

"Well, you're going to be called 'King', aren't you?"

"Bit ordinary. Edward the Confessor and Ethelred the Unready were called 'King', and what a pair of twats they were. I want something a bit alpha male."

"Barbarian?"

"I'm s'posed to be a Christian. That reminds me, I'm going to have to do something to keep the snowflakes happy. They start mithering when I kill too many people."

"Couple of Hail Marys?"

"They like something a bit more concrete than that. I know! I'll build an abbey. Here. We can call that Battle — Battle Abbey."

"Sounds a little — aggressive — for a church?"

"Oh, they won't mind about that, so long as their name's on the deeds. Now, back to my name."

"William the Terminator? William the Great? William the Conqueror?"

"The last one! No, I like that! That'll do! Now, I suppose I'd better go and despoil Harold's body. Promised I'd chuck him into the sea if I won. All in a day's work, I suppose."

"I'm off to see if I can find anything to pillage. See you later!"

Arthur
I
Physics, Space, 13.7 Billion Years BC

There is nothing. All is nothing. A bleak empty cold dark nothingness that is everywhere and nowhere. It extends for ever and has been so for ever. There is no beginning or end, no alpha and omega, no music of the spheres, no God to view the darkness and formlessness of the void. It is beyond comprehension.

Except.

A fragment of matter travelling at the speed of light squared flashes through the emptiness. It has also existed for ever, trekking its solitary path through the void, doomed to continue forever.

It contains all the matter, energy and time that could become a universe, compressed into the size of a marble. It weighs 3.2×10^{54} kg, and is stable. Just. The addition of one nanogram of — well, anything — would be sufficient to tip it into instability.

There is another element in this proto-universe. It is a particle of dust. It too has been zipping along for time immemorial. But it is just a humble piece of dust. It is not special. In 13.4 billion years' time it will be hoovered up by the cleaner.

But it weighs 5.7 nanograms.

The two elements have pursued their separate courses in this infinity of time and space, never having come within a trillion trillion miles of each other. But physics tells us that because they exist in an infinity, at some point they must meet. Because, in an infinity, anything that can happen, will happen.

And so it does.

Aided by gravitational attraction, the smaller particle veers into the course of the larger. They collide at a closing speed of 69,192,000,000 miles per second. The dust crashes to the centre of the marble, generating a heat of four trillion degrees Celsius and tipping the weight to 3.2×10^{54} kg and 4.7 nanograms.

There is a pause of one nanosecond. Then the thing explodes. In the next nanosecond all the matter that makes up the universe is created, every element, all the energy, time itself, and is flung with unimaginable force into the void, to carry on expanding with increasing velocity to create the universe we know today.

The original particles are utterly and completely destroyed. Or almost. A sub atomic fraction of the original marble, still containing all the potential for time, matter and energy, survives, and meets, in the second nanosecond, newly formed elements of carbon, hydrogen, oxygen and nitrogen. It has an affinity for them, and it combines with them to create a unique molecule. This molecule joins the cloud of matter that will condense, several billion years later, to form our galaxy, our sun, our solar system, and our earth. And, ultimately, our primal soup. We shall call it Trevor.

II
Chemistry, Earth, 4 Billion Years BC

Nine billion years have now elapsed, and Trevor is floating around the atmosphere of early Earth. Earth is quite happy with developments so far. It has just celebrated its billionth birthday, and is quite proud of its new atmosphere. It's not an atmosphere that would float our boats, though, consisting as it does of a superheated brew of ammonia, methane, hydrogen sulphide and steam, and racked by constant cataclysmic electrical storms, but it's OK by Trevor.

Down below, however, things are going on. Organic compounds are being formed in the seething mass of solids and fluids that pass for the surface of Earth. Theories abound about the origins of life, but in fact what happens is really quite straightforward. All life is really just a wet bag of nucleic acids joined together and directing other stuff, and one night a particularly violent storm jams together preformed molecules of adenine, thymine, guanine and cytosine. This particular arrangement is self-replicating, so hey presto! — we have life. From that admittedly quite difficult conceptual beginning it is a relatively straightforward process through prokaryotes, archaea and eukaryotes to elephants, Brexit supporters and anti-vaxxers.

For Trevor, already being to all intents and purposes an organic molecule, this is an open goal. He (she?) gravitates towards this biochemical miracle, and in no time at all ingratiates himself into one of these very early genomes. And so, from the very beginnings of life on earth, genetic material exists that has the ability to distort time. Or, to put it in layman's terms, to facilitate time travel.

III
Biology, Earth, 66 Million Years BC

There is a snag, though, not that Trevor is particularly concerned about it. While there is nothing to stop Trevor being passed down from generation to generation, because genetics, and therefore life, has arranged itself in such a way to require *two* of anything to actually achieve anything, and has also quite gratuitously introduced the concept of dominant and recessive genes, Trevor finds himself condemned to the latter category and impotent. He is a recessive gene. Which means he can only express himself if there is another Trevor. Which, given he is the only Trevor in the whole universe, is pretty unlikely.

Or so he thinks.

But in fact, in the midst of the cataclysm that was the Big Bang, exactly eleven other Trevors were created, spread over a space of a trillion trillion trillion cubic miles. This still made the chances of two Trevors meeting one another pretty slim, but as we learnt a bit earlier, in an infinity situation if something *can* happen, it *will* happen.

Around sixty-six million years ago a big asteroid slammed into what is today Mexico, an event affectionately known as the K-Pg extinction. It eliminated three quarters of the animal and plant species on the planet, so could be considered pretty bad news. In doing so it cleared the way for mammals, then man, to become the dominant life form, which again could be considered pretty bad news as man is now busily engaged in replicating the mass extinction of other species, and probably his own. But the good news is that another Trevor was embedded in the asteroid, and was released into the wild by this colossal explosion.

It takes another ten million years for the two Trevors to meet in the double helix that is DNA, but the outcome of that monumental meeting, even more significant than that of Stanley and Livingstone or Kardashian and West, is that for the first time in recorded history a viable organism has an active gene for time travel. And that organism is a mushroom. We have a time travelling mushroom!

Of course, the mushroom, which belongs to a now extinct genus bearing in appearance a remarkable similarity to an elephant's foreskin, is blissfully unaware of its time travels. Neither do the various eras in which it turns up think it particularly remarkable that a mushroom has suddenly appeared in its midst out of the blue.

With one exception.

One afternoon in June 1892 the famous French chef, Auguste Escoffier, was busy in the kitchen of the Savoy Hotel in London. It was a big day. Queen Victoria was coming to tea, and Auguste wanted to impress her. He thought she'd probably want something fairly light before embarking on the gargantuan dinner a couple of hours later that typified the late Victorian and Edwardian period, and so something like mushrooms on toast would do the trick. Of course, being Escoffier, he wouldn't have called it 'mushrooms on toast', but something far more glamorous, but he hadn't thought of a name yet.

A delivery of Covent Garden's best had arrived a couple

of hours earlier, but when he turned to it to create his dish, something odd had happened. Sitting in the middle of the heap of mushrooms was something that looked like an elephant's foreskin. It was not the unusual appearance of this mushroom that excited him, though; it was the scent. He had never smelt anything like it before. It out-truffled the most expensive truffle he had ever encountered. Through his daze he became dimly aware of a dog howling in ecstasy in the distance; it had obviously caught the scent as well.

Escoffier popped outside and gave the dog a piece of the mushroom, just to check it wouldn't kill anyone. The dog lived. It more than lived; it rolled over on its back in an ecstasy of happiness. Escoffier had to drag it by its tail away from the door to get rid of it.

So Escoffier's dilemma on what to give Queen Victoria for her tea was resolved. He constructed an elaborate recipe of mushrooms, cream and garlic, with the novel fungus as its centrepiece. He had only a slight sense of misgiving that she might, too, think it looked like an elephant's foreskin. Accustomed to naming his dishes after the famous, with massive insensitivity given the appearance of the principle attraction, he named it 'Champignon Prince Albert'.

But Queen Victoria was not to be given the chance to be offended by either the appearance or name of the dish. The mushroom had been miffed by being fed in part to a dog, and the moment Escoffier's back was turned transitioned back to the early Cenozoic era. Escoffier had to serve Queen Victoria plain old mushrooms on toast, and she was heard to remark afterwards to her current favourite, Abdul Karim, "If that's the best the bloody Frogs can do, they can sod off back to Paris. I could murder a Ruby tonight."

Sadly, possession of the time travelling gene does not confer immortality, and the mushroom went the way of all flesh. The two Trevors were split by the process of meiosis, and went their separate ways borne on the wind within the spores of their parent mushroom. Neither spore survived, and the Trevors were cast adrift as two simple organic molecules, albeit immensely potentially powerful ones.

Biology is a churn, and the compounds that constitute life have to come from somewhere, and that somewhere is Earth's environment. And so it came to pass (sounding strangely biblical for a moment) that after a mere few million years, Trevor found himself reincorporated into another genome.

It was the genome of a tree shrew.

And the tree shrew is the direct ancestor of all primates. Including man.

IV
Croydon, Sunday, 23rd October, 2016

Arthur Smith was engaged in his favourite Sunday morning activity — moaning. His long-suffering wife, Jill, attempting to read the Observer, gave up.

"I really don't know why you're being so miserable about your birthday, Arthur," said Jill. "It's not as if it's a big one. Anyway, they say fifty-four is the new thirty-four."

"I don't feel thirty-four. If anything, I feel bloody sixty-four. And I think I'm going bald."

"Well, if you didn't sit and stuff in that armchair all day... Come on, the kids said they'd treat you to a steak."

"First of all, you accuse me of sitting and stuffing myself to death, then you invite me for unidentifiable animal and chips at that bloody awful place on the roundabout. I can't win!"

"I wish you wouldn't say 'bloody' so much. They did say, if the steak house offended your fine dining sensibilities, we could go to the Jewel of Bengal instead. Apparently, it's under new ownership and they're trying a 'cuisine minceur'."

"Terrific. You pay more for less but still get the same old food poisoning."

"At least that would keep your weight down. I'll take that as a yes."

"I'll need to check my diary."

"What! When was the last time you went out in the

evening? By yourself? Apart from your beermat activities? And you count down the days to those."

"Do you know the most interesting thing about my birthday?"

"Yes. You tell me every year. But don't let that stop you."

"I was born in the middle of the Cuban Missile Crisis. Mum had me at home and insisted she deliver under the living room table in case an H-bomb went off in mid push. And that's why my middle name is John; Mum was so grateful to Kennedy for not pushing the button. Dad suggested, in fairness we include Nikita as well, but Mum said I'd never get a job in the civil service if they did that."

"Maybe she had a point. I'll ring the kids to tell them we're on for Thursday before you change your mind."

"And do you know what else is really interesting?"

"I'm going to ring the kids."

"No, this is *really* interesting."

"I'm not going to escape, am I?"

"We seem to have a family link with H-bombs. My mum worked out once, she was conceived on the same day as the first atomic bomb test in July 1945."

"Was that the elusive Yank boyfriend that made your grandma hate Americans for ever afterwards?"

"The same."

"Can I ring now?"

Jill exited the room, to find the one spot upstairs in the little three-bedroom semi where she could get phone reception. She might not have been interested in Arthur's meanderings, but in fact what he had said was very interesting indeed.

V
Croydon, 16th July, 1945

Trevor had been dutifully passing himself down the genome of evolution. From tree shrews through things that looked like cute little kangaroos to the very early primates and hence to man. The 16th July, 1945 found Trevor sitting in the genome of Arthur's grandmother, Mildred. Still alone. And still impotent as a recessive gene.

But two fairly monumental things happened on the 16th July, 1945. Firstly, Arthur's grandmother finally (she'd held out for two whole days) succumbed to the blandishments of US Army Private First-Class Hiram H. Ledbetter, whom she'd met at a dance the previous Saturday. The gift of five tins of Spam and two packets of Lucky Strike had by no means harmed the private's case.

Of possibly even more significance that day was the explosion of the world's first atomic bomb in a test carried out in a desert somewhere in the United States. The bomb had a yield equivalent to about twenty kilotons of TNT; peanuts compared to today's monsters, but still quite impressive for the time. Nuclear weapons depend on initiating chain reactions, and one of the things the scientists who'd developed the thing were a teensy bit worried about, was that the chain reaction necessary for the successful operation of the bomb might actually extend to the Earth as a whole, and vaporise the entire planet. So they heaved a bit of a sigh of relief when not only did the bomb go bang as it was supposed to, it did not destroy the planet.

There was an unnoticed effect, though. The two Trevors had always had a weak affinity for one another, a by-product of their unique chemistry. Up until now, that affinity had only been effective over a few metres or so, and so had had little impact on our story. The shock of the atomic bomb had indeed sent ripples through the atmosphere of earth as a whole, and one of the consequences was that it increased the affinity of the two particles for each other a trillion-fold. Trevor Number One was lodged inside Arthur's grandmother, and therefore immobilised, but Trevor Number Two, who had just emerged from a rotting tree in the Brazilian rain forest, sniffed the air, rapidly calculated his latitude and longitude, and came hurtling over to Croydon.

Given the incredible accuracy required to hit a back alley in Croydon from Brazil, Trevor No. 2 could perhaps be forgiven for slamming into Private Ledbetter's body, specifically his Y chromosome, rather than directly joining Trevor No. 1. But given the intricacies of mammalian sex, this was just what was needed for the two Trevors to conjoin in Mildred. And so the two Trevors were reunited after a gap of some fifty million years.

Mildred had only the loosest idea of the facts of life, and whilst understanding that human reproduction required a male and a female to get reasonably close to one another, she had been assured by her peer group that hopping in a circle three times after the event was a sure-fire way to prevent anything untoward happening. Indeed, PFC Ledbetter had been quite unsettled by this behaviour, believing that correct post coital conduct was to have a fag, though preferably in a luxurious

Hollywood bed rather than a back alley in Croydon. So, it came as some surprise to Mildred some six months later to find that her swelling tummy was not due to a surfeit of Spam, but to a baby girl.

The two Trevors now hit a snag. Their only previous expression had been in the time travelling mushroom, and mushrooms are single sex. There is no lady mushroom and no gentleman mushroom. But in humankind there are (at time of writing) two official sexes, as defined by the XY (male) and XX (female) chromosomes, and the two Trevors were inhibited by the XX chromosome combination. Given Mildred's first (and only) born was a girl, the Trevors had to sit out another twenty odd years until they could express their potential, free of constraint, in the XY chromosome embryo that was to become Arthur.

VI
Croydon, October 2016

Arthur had been feeling distinctly odd. It seemed to date from the day of his fifty-fourth birthday. He had at first put it down to his evening at the Jewel of Bengal, when his two children, Stevyn and Kate, had generously offered to pay for the whole meal, drinks included, to the value of ten pounds per head. Working within this budget had led to a degree of compromise on his choice of dishes, but the waiter had been very enthusiastic about the offal thali, very reasonably priced mainly because nobody else would touch it with a bargepole. He had struggled through most of the little dishes that would probably have offended the inhabitants of Leningrad at the height of their siege, and had duly spent a restless night while his digestive system attempted to cope with the novel task demanded of it. But the after effects of the meal lasted little more than three days, and a couple of weeks later he was still feeling something was not quite right.

He started having weird dreams. Not the usual confusion of never being where he should be and if he was not, knowing what he was supposed to be doing there, compounded by whatever was going wrong being at height. Or hunting fruitlessly for a toilet, or even the very occasional dream where he found himself in a potentially compromising situation with Mrs Frobisher, the head of H.R., although in truth these happy rarities generally morphed into something to do with toilets, or heights, or being lost, or sometimes all three at once.

No. His dreams were of historical events. They were vivid, and memorable, and when he checked one against Wikipedia, surprisingly accurate. Now, Arthur had never taken much interest in history. In fact, he had never taken very much interest in anything, with one great exception. He had been dutiful at school, and had emerged with A Levels in English, French and Geography, subjects chosen, well, really, on the basis of no grounds whatsoever. They had been sufficient to get him into one of the newer universities, from which he had graduated with a second class (upper division) degree in English. In such a university it took considerable skill to achieve a lower qualification. This degree took him into the civil service, the Department of Agriculture to be precise, where he had remained ever since.

If Arthur was such a nonentity, why, one might reasonably ask oneself, had he managed to attract such a nice, and it must be said attractive, lady as Jill to be his wife? Well. Despite Arthur's confusion at the onset of puberty — he had no idea why a very muddled dream in which Suzi Quattro had briefly figured should have led to wet pyjamas — and his total incomprehension at his schoolmates' (friends is much too strong a word) enthusiasm about girls, by the end of his teens he was actually not bad looking, and was attracting female attention. This attraction was amplified by his general air of bewilderment in any kind of social environment, particularly to those girls of a kindly nature. Jill was one such girl. They had become acquainted towards the end of her second and his third year at university, and an end of year barn dance had been the catalyst for their relationship. She had just emerged from a relationship in which her partner had let her down, and she was

26

looking for someone more reliable and with rather less ego. As Arthur had no ego whatsoever, he seemed a perfect choice. That was the official version anyway. Arthur was adamant they had met briefly at the beginning of the year, but try as she might, Jill had no memory of that. In fact, Jill's memories of that whole period were sometimes a little — opaque.

Arthur wondered if it was his age. That there was some secret that no one had ever told him about turning fifty-four. A bit like when on his thirteenth birthday he had had that wet dream. Or a year later when his voice suddenly went totally out of control. There was nobody he knew, or at least men of his age group, he could discuss it with because, to put it bluntly, he didn't have any friends. There was the Croydon Beermat Society, of which he was an avid and lifelong member, but the idea of a personal conversation at one of its monthly meetings, even with someone he'd known for more than thirty years, was unthinkable.

In fact, it was Arthur's age. Life in general, and human life in particular, is governed by the clock. Growth is completed (or at least upward growth) by the late teens. Fertility, as experienced by Arthur, is endowed in the early teens. Hair starts going grey too soon. And then you die. But within Arthur there was another artefact governed by the clock. And a very strict clock. The Trevors were timed to turn on at the precise fifty- fourth anniversary of Arthur's birth, and turn on they did, although their effect did not go immediately to plan because of the struggle his insides were having with the offal curry. But shortly after Arthur's fifth visit to the toilet, they had seized control.

Apocalypse Then

I
London, January 1066

"Edie! Babe! Don't take on so!"

Edith the Swan-neck most definitely, and probably justifiably to the modern eye, had the hump. Her partner of twenty odd years and father of her six children, Harold Godwinson, now King Harold II of England, had decided as a matter of political expediency to marry someone else. Long tipped to take over from the heirless Edward the Confessor, the crunch point had arrived in early January 1066 when the old boy had died. His body was barely cold before Harold had had himself crowned in Westminster Abbey. But not everybody was happy. In fact, very few people were happy, hence Harold's decision to marry power in the shape of Ealdgyth of Mercia and her murderous, yet very influential, connections. So far as he was concerned it was a marriage of expediency, and nothing to do with her legendary beauty. But Edith didn't see it that way.

"I thought we were supposed to be married?"

"We are, babe, we are," mumbled Harold, unconvincingly.

"Then how come the Church allowed you to marry this — tart — in Westminster Abbey?"

Edith had recently learnt that Ealdgyth was the grand-daughter of the infamous Lady Godiva, and she certainly wasn't going to let that one go.

Harold shifted uncomfortably.

"Well, the Archbish of Canterbury, you know, old Stigand, said there wouldn't be a problem because — er, because…"

"Because what?" screeched Edith.

"Er, because," Harold took a deep breath. "Because the Church doesn't really count, er, what we did, as the real thing."

"What?" yelled Edith again. "You told me, that all we had to do was shake hands and that would be that, proper marriage. You were just trying to get up my skirt!"

Edith was referring to 'Danish Marriage', or the 'hand fasting' ceremony, a fairly widespread practice at the time, but one that the Church considered left the groom free to marry properly, that is under Christian ceremony, at a later date. Harold had omitted to mention this to Edith. And yes, he had wanted to get up her skirt.

"Well, it's done now," said Harold, grumpily. "You'll just have to put up with it. And it strengthens my position. Reduces the chances of having my head stuck on a spear on London Bridge. I thought you'd be pleased with that."

"Yes, I'm sure she'll do all sorts of things for your position," retorted Edith. "But don't come running back to me when you've got her up the spout and she's not at home to your — bestiality!"

"You didn't seem to mind my bestiality before," murmured Harold.

"What!?"

Harold tried to draw the — painful — conversation to a close. He was very fond of Edith, and pushing forty and with all those children behind her she was still an attractive woman. But politics were politics, even if in this particular case the sacrifice was considerably alleviated by Ealdgyth's skills in the bedroom.

"I'm sure we'll find a way through," he said.

"Well, I will," muttered Edith, darkly.

II
Falaise, Normandy, January 1066

"Those Cnuts!" shrieked William.

The messenger shifted uncomfortably from foot to foot.

"The Cnuts!" William shrieked again.

"Bad news?" asked Matilda. "And I do wish you wouldn't use that kind of language, especially in front of the children."

The children in question, Robert and William, sniggered together in the corner of the main hall of Falaise Castle.

"Ma's going really deaf," tittered Robert, to his younger brother. "Pa's probably never heard of the word she thinks he said, and he's too God-fearing to say it anyway."

His brother didn't really know what he was talking about, but went along with it anyway. It was safer.

"What is it, anyway?" asked Matilda again. "Your face is really red."

"It's that bastard, Harold! Harold bloody Godwinson! He's crowned himself King of England!" William glared at the unhappy messenger as if it was all his fault.

"Can I go now, please, sir; my round finishes at one o'clock, and the wife gets anxious if I'm late," ventured the messenger. William dismissed him with an angry wave.

"He is English. Nobody trusts them," said Matilda, placatingly. "Why are you so upset?"

"Because he promised it to me! Two years ago, the bastard, when he was over here!"

"I seem to remember you had a good time together," Matilda said mildly. "I expect it was just the beer talking. What do you want England for? It's a cold, miserable place. You've got Normandy, and if you get bored with that there's always Belgium, through me." Matilda considered she owned Belgium, and that it was within her gift to offer it as a kind of back garden to William when he was in one of his moods. In fact, as a direct descendant of the Kings of France, she was probably in a position to offer even more than Belgium. But she didn't like to rub it in that she was more highly born than her husband.

"I'm not going to let him get away with this!" William was no calmer. "Just because he's related — very distantly I might add! — to King Cnut, he thinks he can bloody well do what he wants. Once a Cnut, always a Cnut! I've got just as much right as he has! My grandad was Edward the Confessor's uncle!"

"Neither of you seem to have that direct a claim," Matilda pointed out.

"Oh, here we go! You can't let it drop, can you, that I'm William the Bastard and you're Matilda of bloody Flanders, granddaughter of the King of France. Well, I want England and I'm bloody going to get England!"

"Yes dear," said Matilda, meekly.

III
London, September 1066

Harold's fears for his position were proving well founded (those, that is, related to his political rivals, not anything to do with his new bride. No fears there).

"Christ almighty," he moaned to his brother, Gyrth. "God knows why William is taking this all so seriously. He's got Normandy and half of Belgium anyway."

"You did promise him," ventured Gyrth. "When you toured France in '64."

"That was under duress."

"What, the duress of too many bottles of the local vino?"

"No, under the duress of being shipwrecked in France, being captured by that twat, Guy of Ponce-moi, or whatever..."

"Guy, Count of Ponthieu," corrected Gyrth.

"Whatever, he's a mercenary twat. He sold me to William!"

"And William forced you to go on the piss with him?"

"Well, I must admit it was a good night."

"And you promised him England in return for a good night out?"

"It wasn't like that at all. It was this drinking game he wanted to play. If he lost, I got France, and if I lost, he got England. I must admit I was a bit fuzzy about the rules, but I never thought he'd take it seriously. Anyway, whose side are

33

you on?" Harold countered, aggressively.

"And what about Harald? Hardrada?"

Harold sunk his head into his hands.

"I know which Harald you mean. He's nothing but a bleeding pirate."

"He might be a bleeding pirate, but he's got fifteen thousand big hairy Vikings in three hundred ships ready to hit Tyneside."

Harold groaned.

"He has no right to the throne, either. Just because the Danes did some shady deal with each other back in ancient history, they think they can walk back in whenever they want."

"With fifteen thousand lust crazed Vikings, all intent on the rape and pillage of our delicate Geordie maidens…"

"The same maidens who are out on the piss every Friday night in the freezing cold in the shortest tunics I've ever seen?"

"…they probably can."

"Any idea what William can bring to the party?"

Gyrth consulted a parchment he had brought in with him.

"According to our spies, he's gathered about seven hundred ships and ten thousand men opposite Sussex. Although some sources say one and a half million men."

"Oh Christ," moaned Harold.

"There are rumours he's infiltrating *his* spies over here. Dressed as nuns. People in the South are getting panicky, and there are reports of nuns being burnt for talking French. Given the peasantry don't have a clue what French sounds like, that's any poor woman who's got a slightly different accent from their own. In fact, I now hear they're going for *anyone* who looks or sounds slightly different."

"What *is* the state of our army? At this particular point in time?"

Gyrth consulted the parchment again.

"Brace yourself."

Harold groaned again.

"Four hundred and ninety-four men, and three officers."

"But — I left about ten thousand in the Isle of Wight. Only a couple of weeks ago."

"None of the French you promised them showed up, and they felt their time was better spent back on their farms. So they all went home. Apart from the five hundred or so who stayed."

"At least they're loyal."

"They're also mostly criminals who joined up as part of that amnesty you declared. They feel safer on the Isle of Wight than back home, even if the French turn up."

"They'll get their Frogs all right — just don't know whether it'll be before or after the sex crazed Vikings. For Christ's sake get everyone back together."

"OK, boss," said Gyrth, and went off to try and find the army.

IV
London, Summer 1066

Edith was feeling distinctly unsettled. She had just turned forty, and while this was well in excess of average life expectancy in eleventh century England, she was, as Harold had observed, still a good-looking woman, and she was missing male company. Despite the fuss she'd made at Harold's announcement of his marriage, she was a realist who knew that England's future in general, and her future in particular, rested on Harold's body parts not being separately displayed on London Bridge. That did not stop her from feeling deeply hacked off at Harold's behaviour, and wishing for some kind of revenge.

She contemplated an affair. The problem was with whom, and how. At court she was surrounded by attractive young men, but if they were not deterred by the fact of her relationship with Harold, they would view sex with a forty-year-old woman as virtual necrophilia. In short, they valued their bollocks over a bit of ancient totty. And if she actually did manage to attract someone, where would they go? There wasn't a lot of privacy in the sort of hall that formed the substance of a typical Anglo-Saxon home.

In truth, Edith wasn't really attracted to these young men, gorgeous eye candy as they were. She wanted someone she could talk to, not immature airheads whose only topic of conversation was war and, when not war, the latest court talent contest or who had scored what in the premier league of mob football. Harold was a big, strapping, handsome man who had been quite fun in years gone by, but was now weighed down by ambition and affairs of state. She wanted someone *different*, but with no real idea of who that might be.

But Edith wasn't the kind of woman to give up easily. And despite the fact that the court would soon be emptied of nubile young men as England prepared for war, that in itself would present its own opportunities.

V
London, Tuesday, 9th May, 2017

Arthur was becoming increasingly bothered by his dreams, which had now been going on for several months. They were intruding on reality. He usually spent his half hour journey from Croydon East into Charing Cross in a state of total abstraction, maybe desultorily leafing through a Metro, or gazing out at the increasingly grim terraced housing that backed onto the rubbish strewn railway line as it entered the heart of the capital. But one day, about half way into his journey as he was staring blankly out of the train window, there was no terraced housing. Instead, there were green fields dotted with clumps of huts. He blinked and rubbed his eyes. The familiar bleak terraces reappeared. He must have fallen briefly asleep, he reasoned, except that two days later the same thing happened.

Arthur usually enjoyed his walk from Charing Cross to his office at the Ministry of Agriculture in Smith Square, and back in the evening. In fact, when the sleet was not horizontal, he regarded it as pretty well the best part of his day. But on the morning of Tuesday, 9th May, 2017, as he emerged from Whitehall, he saw not the usual chaos of competing protest movements but an expanse of muddy green fields, marked only by a large wooden hall by the riverside surrounded by a few huts of the type he'd seen from his train window, and an imposing looking stone structure webbed by wooden scaffolding, obviously in a state of construction. Tiny figures clad in rough tunics and leggings swung perilously from the framework, while at ground level more workmen scurried to and fro. Returning his bewildered gaze to the hall, similarly clad but helmeted and armed men were posted around the outside. He slowly turned round. Modern London had disappeared, to be replaced by clusters of huts dotted haphazardly around endless muddy fields.

He turned back to face the hall, and was alarmed to see two helmeted figures armed with extremely imposing axes advancing towards him. He froze to the spot like a rabbit caught in headlights.

"Morning, sir," said the more frightening of the two figures as they halted in front of him. "Can we help you?"

Now the two soldiers, and everyone else inhabiting the eleventh century in this narrative, obviously did not speak modern English. They spoke Old English, which had developed from Anglo Frisian or Ingvaeonic dialects spoken by the Germanic tribes that had invaded England during the Dark Ages. So, to Arthur's ear 'Good Morning' would have sounded like 'Godne Mergen', (which actually isn't a hundred miles away from modern English. A deeper conversation would have posed far greater difficulties). But this narrative would grind to a halt if all the places Arthur is to visit demanded communication in their own language. So, engaging a degree of poetic licence, the *lingua franca* of this account will be modern English.

Arthur could not answer. He was terrified. His perceptions of reality had been ripped apart. He stood gaping at the soldiers like a landed fish.

"Would you mind coming with us, sir?"

This was not a request. Arthur found himself flanked by the two soldiers, and through his panic understood that if he did not propel himself forward, it would be done for him. He was semi frogmarched to a small hut immediately adjacent to the Great Hall, where an even more intimidating military man sat behind a rough desk.

"Morning, Sarge," said Chad, for that was the name of the less frightening of his two guards. "Caught this one copping our troop strengths around the palace."

The sergeant looked Arthur up and down with disgust. Despite the fact that Arthur had not as yet uttered a word, his unique garb of Marks and Sparks plain dark suit, white shirt and blue tie, had immediately marked him out as a Norman spy.

"He can join those two nuns we caught earlier on."

Arthur's gaze followed his outstretched arm towards the crude window. To his horror, he saw two pairs of sandaled feet dangling just outside, the property of two unfortunate Irish nuns, Sisters Dolores and Kathleen, who, on hearing a brand-new abbey was being built in the centre of London, had come on a special sightseeing trip to admire the wonder at first hand.

"Come on, squire," said Chad, gruffly, as he seized Arthur's arm. "Any last words?"

Arthur managed to find something resembling a voice. "You've made a mistake. Please! A terrible mistake!" he squeaked.

The trio of officers paused. Now, despite the fact, as discussed earlier, they were all talking the same language, Arthur definitely had an accent that differed from theirs.

"You see," said the sergeant. "French. He's definitely a Frog."

Chad's companion, Cuthbert, now chimed in. Cuthbert was the more highly educated of the two, having entered the sixth form at his school and stayed on till the age of seven. "He sounds quite posh, though."

The other two paused at this observation.

"He does," said Chad. "Maybe he's an officer. Or nobility."

"Or William himself," chipped in the sergeant. This was wildly speculative, as no one in England had the least idea of what William looked like. But they suspected he looked foreign.

"Maybe we should pass this up the line," suggested Cuthbert, cautiously. "We don't want to hang someone we shouldn't." Nuns did not fall into this category.

The other two nodded. They felt they had the authority to hang ordinary passers-by, but not someone who might be more important than them.

"Let's do that," said the sergeant. "Just to be on the safe side."

Up the line was, in fact, Edith. It was midsummer 1066, and Harold was away touring the length and breadth of England grubbing together an army. Ealdgyth had just given birth, and was far too absorbed with her new son, Harold junior, to take any interest in the affairs of state. Edith, as the long-term partner of Harold, had accumulated quite a lot of experience in administration, and despite their tensions over his connubial arrangements, he had trusted her enough to run the country in his absence.

Administering the Kingdom was actually not all that onerous — an execution here and a branding there — and the court was virtually empty, so Edith was passing the time doing a little tapestry work when she became aware of a commotion at the entrance to the Great Hall. Two of the men at arms she recognised as Chad and Cuthbert were marching a strangely clad figure towards her. They halted in front of her with a great crashing of boots.

"Morning, ma'am," said Chad, on behalf of all three of them.

Edith gazed at the figure standing miserably between them. She had never seen anyone — or anything — so exotic in her life.

"Who's this," she asked, a slight tremor in her voice.

"Frenchie spy, ma'am," replied Chad. "We caught 'im creeping around outside. Obvs. assessing our strengths and capabilities. We was going to 'ang 'im there and then, but then he opens 'is gob and he talks real funny, all la-de-da like. So we thinks he might be important, so we thinks we'd better not 'ang him till we've spoken to you, 'cos 'e might be important. Ma'am." Chad had rarely strung so many thoughts together at one go.

Edith addressed Arthur, "What have you got to say for yourself?"

"There's been a terrible mistake. I'm Arthur Smith and I'm a civil servant. I don't know what on earth's going on. But I'm sorry if I've upset anyone."

Now there has been some debate as to whether there is a distinctive Croydon accent. Whatever the pros and cons of that argument, the dialect that Arthur spoke was impossibly smooth and refined compared to the guttural tones of his Anglo-Saxon escorts, and Edith was smitten. Not only was his attire the most glamorous she'd ever seen, his speech like honey to her ear, his general appearance radiating health (a slight belly on a man was well regarded then as a sign of wealth and good living), but he was tall (compared to his Anglo-Saxon companions), and still had vestiges of his youthful good looks despite a fair degree of hair loss. This sign of human frailty endeared him even more to Edith. She managed to calm her fluttering heart enough to say, "Leave him here. I'll interrogate him. Good work, men."

Chad and Cuthbert basked in Edith's acclaim. "Thank you, ma'am," they exclaimed simultaneously, and turning smartly on their heels they clumped out.

She turned to Arthur with a shy smile on her face. "I'm Edith," she said. "Edith the Swan-neck. Queen of England." She felt complicated explanations of her actual status were unnecessary at this point. After all, she was to all intents and purposes Queen. At least for the moment. "Who are you? Really?"

Arthur regarded the woman sitting on a fairly plain wooden stool with a length of tapestry on her knee in front of him. She certainly didn't look like his idea of a queen. But Edith, as pointed out previously, was pretty well preserved, and while forty was viewed as almost geriatric in the eleventh century, she was actually some fourteen years younger than Arthur. He felt he could open up to her, although he still had no idea what he was doing there.

"I'm Arthur," he began, hesitantly.

"A noble name!" interjected Edith, gazing adoringly at him.

"Er, thank you. I come from a place called Croydon. It's part of London."

Never had a place name sounded so mysterious yet so desirable to her.

"Croy-don," she repeated, slowly, savouring the way the syllables glided off her tongue.

Arthur had never met that reaction to his home town before. It was usually a snigger. He felt himself warming to Edith.

"I don't know how I got here," he continued. "I thought I might be dreaming at first." But that illusion had been shattered when he saw the two dangling nuns. "I don't know, but it seems like some kind of time travel." Incredulous as the idea was to Arthur, which he promptly dismissed and forgot, he had hit the nail on the head.

The idea of time travel was so much gobbledegook to Edith, but being of her time she was a firm believer in magic, and so was quite happy to accept 'time travel' as an aspect of the occult she was heretofore unfamiliar with. So far as she was concerned, it just added to Arthur's attraction.

"Tell me more," she breathed.

So Arthur did.

VI
London, September 1066

Edith was in love. She had never known anything like it. She had loved her big, strong, impetuous Harold right from the beginning, but even that had been a marriage, or non-marriage, of convenience, her wealthy land-owning father allying himself with the politically powerful Godwinson family. But she was enchanted by this mysterious stranger who entertained her night after night with incredible tales of things to come — a time when the country would be run by the people and not powerful warlords, ships would sail through the air to the other side of the world and people would talk to each other a hundred miles away with little black things they kept in their pockets. Arthur had shown her his mobile phone, and while the battery lasted, she had been enchanted with the wonders it could perform — it could add up numbers, tell the time and most fantastic and unbelievable of all — take pictures. Of course, being the eleventh century and there being no internet access, Arthur couldn't demonstrate even more wonders like ordering your shopping from Tesco's, watching endless clips of cute animals on YouTube and how teenage girls could intimidate each other via social media.

Arthur, for his part, had simply decided to go with the flow. Edith had installed him in one of the posher huts next to the Great Hall, and while during the day he would sit with her in the Hall, evenings — and the occasional night — were spent round at his. He enjoyed being with Edith — it was certainly preferable to being strung up outside the Hall, or even an average day at the office — and when the relationship went rather beyond what either of them had expected, he felt no qualms. Given his best estimate of what was going on was that he was dreaming, and he had felt no guilt about Suzi Quattro or, indeed, Mrs. Frobisher from HR, why should he feel he was cheating with a medieval queen?

For Edith, though, it was an entirely different kettle of fish. Eleventh century morality was pretty strict, and the Church forbad any kind of liaison outside of marriage. Added to that, men like Harold wanted to make damn sure that any offspring were theirs, given that in the Middle Ages the fruit of one's own loins could be pretty dangerous, let alone the fruit of anyone else's. She felt her position was reasonably safe, though. Harold was a long way away, and she could trust the ladies of the court, if only because they were missing their menfolk too and some had come to alternative arrangements with such males as were left.

But Edith had not reckoned on the soldiery. She regarded the soldiers guarding the Great Hall, who had been largely recruited from the peasantry, as one might a friendly bovine animal, put on earth to serve a particular purpose but with little understanding of the world around it. So, if a guard had spotted her shadowy figure flitting around the outside of the Hall of a night-time, she thought nothing of it. But Chad and Cuthbert and their sarge had felt a bit miffed by Edith's treatment of Arthur. Whilst denied the pleasure of hanging him themselves for the perfectly understandable reason they may have got a bollocking for terminating someone more important than them, they had rather expected Arthur to have been dealt with rather more severely than being given his own hut and the undivided and suspicious attention of the Queen. They moaned to each other, they moaned to their mates, their mates moaned to other mates, and pretty soon the whole army knew that *something* was going on.

VII
North of London, September, 1066

Harold's brother, Gyrth, had just left him after a general review of the strategic situation, which overall was not too bad. They had just returned from the North where they had taken out Harald Hardrada's army at Stamford Bridge, and were now encamped just outside London.

"Nice one, Harold," said Gyrth. "Shame about Tostig, though." He was referring to the death of their brother in the battle, who had taken Hardrada's side.

"I don't know," said Harold. "He was a slimy little toe rag. Always used to pinch my toys."

Gyrth shifted uncomfortably. He and Tostig had both enjoyed bullying Harold as children. He decided to change the subject.

"But William is just about to set sail. Waiting for good omens or something."

"What, a frog with three legs?" Harold sniggered at his own wit. "We've got half our army left. No probs!"

His brother now had to impart the news he had been dreading.

"Er, just one other thing, old chap." He hesitated.

"Come on, man, spit it out!" said Harold, jovially.

"Er, it's Edith."

Harold paused. "Yeeees?" He obviously had had other things on his mind recently, but he was suddenly reminded of

Edith's unhappiness at his connubial arrangements and her veiled threats. "Go on."

Gyrth gulped. "Rumour has it she's been carrying on with a Frenchie spy. And the whole army knows about it."

That explained some of the curious glances he'd received, and the abruptly terminated conversations at his appearance.

Harold went puce. He was incandescent with rage. "I'm off to London. Now!" he bellowed.

VIII
London, October 1066

Gyrth and Edith, as siblings-in-law, had known each other for as long as she and Harold had been married, and they were good friends. He now managed to get word to Edith ahead of Harold's arrival in London of his mood, if that's not too weak a word for the towering rage he was still in. Edith, who had been having intimations of mortality so far as her relationship with Arthur went, acted swiftly. Her ladies in waiting had been broadly sympathetic with her affair, and her favourite had offered a refuge with her family in a nice quiet part of the Sussex countryside near Hastings. So, Arthur had been packed off post haste, and Edith girded her loins to face the music with Harold.

The reunion did not go well. Edith had decided that attack, and lying, was the best form of defence, and Harold was confronted with a barrage of accusations about leaving her vulnerable to the machinations of French spies. In accommodating Arthur, she was doing her best to protect herself and her ladies from the widely known vile and inhuman carnal habits of the French, while he was off galivanting around the summertime freshness of the English countryside. When he pointed out he was actually protecting English womanhood from fifteen thousand blood crazed Vikings who put the French in the shade when it came to bestiality, he was simply told, 'Well, you would say that, wouldn't you!' Harold gave up. On his way back to London he'd been informed that William had landed with a large army on the Sussex coast, which rather put this tiff in the shade, and he knew he wouldn't win with Edith anyway. But he had a pretty good description of Arthur's rather unique appearance, and vowed to himself that if he ever came across him — well!

Events were now accelerating and coalescing towards the dénouement that would determine the next thousand years of English, if not British or even world, history. Of course, Harold didn't know that. This would just be yet another battle, one of many that had formed his experience to date, and one he was quite confident of winning. My goodness, if he'd seen off fifteen thousand Vikings, a few Frogs would be a doddle.

He had gathered together an army of about eight thousand men, largely composed of local levies known as fyrds, but with a backbone of housecarls, his own personal shock troops. The army was short on archers and had no cavalry, but relied on the enemy battering themselves to pieces on the solid defensive shield wall that formed the core of Anglo-Saxon battlefield tactics.

Harold's intelligence services had established that William had thrown up a hurried castle near Hastings, and had based his army there. The English army set off in convoy towards the coast, mounted housecarls at the fore, then the infantry and axemen, and finally the service personnel, doctors, food wagons, astrologers, bloggers, and the wives and girlfriends who viewed the whole event as an exciting excursion with the promise of cakes and ale at the close. The wives and girlfriends included Edith, who thought she had better show some support for Harold and had commandeered the most impressive and comfortable wagon available.

Arthur was rather enjoying his sojourn in Sussex. His hosts had been most hospitable, almost as fascinated by Arthur as Edith had been, and he had free run of the house and its extensive grounds. On the morning of 13th October, he heard a distant commotion over the other side of the slight ridge that formed the boundary of his host's estate. He climbed to the top, to be met with the full panoply of an army on the move. Horse's bridles jangled, banners flew, wagon wheels creaked, and men shouted, against a background of the steady tramp, tramp, tramp of feet. Arthur stood there enchanted by the sight.

Edith was also enjoying the journey, when to her horror, on the crest of a low rise to her right, she spotted a familiar figure, resplendent in Marks and Spencer's suit and white shirt, standing in full view of the army as a whole.

"Christ alive!" she exclaimed. Then, "Go and get him!" to Chad and Cuthbert, who had been recruited as her personal escorts. The two were only too glad to be involved in the retrieval, hoping that long delayed justice would finally catch up with Arthur. They dashed up the slope, grabbed Arthur, and unceremoniously bundled him into the back of Edith's wagon, which, being the most regal cart in the whole royal garage, was covered. Edith prayed that no one else had spotted the incident.

"You idiot!" she hissed at Arthur.

Arthur was yet again bewildered by the turn of events. One minute he had been enjoying what was almost a circus like spectacle, next his twin nemeses of Chad and Cuthbert had dumped him in the back of a horse cart, and Edith was screaming at him.

"Sorry," he mumbled weakly.

IX
Sussex, 14th October, 1066

The battle lines were drawn. The English forces were lined up on Senlac Hill in a dense mass, their front protected by an almost impregnable shield wall, their flanks secured by woody and marshy ground.

William gazed up at his opponents on the high ground above him. He had to destroy this force to progress his invasion, and he was by no means confident. He was a good military commander, and he recognised the strength of the English position, and respected their reputation as defensive fighters. In addition, morale was low amongst his forces. They had found the food in England vile, the wet, cold and windy mid-autumn weather very different from that of their sunny homes, and the women, who all had bad teeth anyway, distinctly unwelcoming. They could not understand why their boss wanted this miserable dump of a country, and sometimes William wondered himself.

The battle opened with the Norman archers launching their arrows at the English position. But, given the angle of the ground, most flew harmlessly over English heads. Their assault soon petered out because the English had few archers themselves, and the French were relying on the return of arrows to keep their own barrage going. They slunk off, demoralised, to the rear.

Next up were the spearmen, but after the long uphill

climb, they were exhausted, and easily repelled, with awful slaughter, by the shield wall. They streamed, broken, back down the hill. Shouts of 'bugger moi, je suis chez moi', were heard from the Norman ranks, together with derisive 'piss off then you cheese eating surrender monkeys!' from the English.

William tried to halt the rout, but the flood of desperate and frightened Normans was so forceful he was knocked off his horse. His temporary disappearance immediately sparked a rumour that he had been killed, which deepened French despair. They streamed away from the battlefield.

The English had won! William was vanquished and the threat to the English succession had been obliterated. For the next thousand years England would be Scandinavian in character, avoiding ruinous European wars and never inflicting upon the world the horrors of imperialism, the Englishman happy with his diet of pickled herring, his hygge, his saunas and his welfare state in which the better off were happy to pay more than fifty percent of their hard-earned income in taxes. Harold gazed with satisfaction at the carnage in front of him, the heaps of Norman dead, with only the odd gap in his own shield wall hacked open by his enemy.

Arthur had lain cowering in the back of Edith's wagon, terrified at the tumult of battle going on around him. But his bladder was at bursting point, and when he heard the sounds of battle subsiding and the shouts of English triumph, he decided he had no option but to take a chance if he was not to add to the general stench of horse manure and decaying wood in the back of Edith's wagon. He cautiously emerged, blinking, into the sunlight.

Unfortunately, Edith, for safety, had parked her cart in the middle of the English position. Harold had full view of Arthur as he emerged.

"There he is!" shrieked Harold. "The French shagger! Seize him!" Half a dozen housecarls launched themselves towards him.

The full horror of Arthur's position hit him like a mailed fist. He stared desperately around him, and saw, not ten yards to his front, a gap in the shield wall. He threw himself forward, breached the wall, and raced off down the hillside with half the English army in pursuit.

William turned from his retreat to watch the extraordinary spectacle unfolding before him. The English position, which a moment ago had been so solid, had now broken, and was racing downhill with a balding man clad in strange black and white clothing at its head. William, as has been said previously, was a good soldier and tactician. He suddenly saw his opportunity, a last desperate throw of the dice. He had not committed his cavalry to the general bloodbath on the hill, but now instructed them to wheel on the English, and his remaining archers to fire on the now much easier target.

The English were caught in the rear, and decimated. William managed to rally his retreating forces, and within minutes the field was his. Victory had been snatched from the jaws of defeat, and as a bonus, Harold had copped an arrow in his eye.

The Norman supremacy was assured. Of the baldy bloke in the black and white costume, there was no sign.

In the Beginning

I
The Cosmos, Eternity

God was bored. God, was God bored! He was terminally bored. He'd managed to keep himself sort of occupied and amused for the last 13.4 billion years or so creating the universe, and there was no doubt he'd felt a sense of achievement when he'd spun a galaxy out of a bit of space dust and not much else. But when you've done a billion or so of them, it did begin to pall a little. His interest had revived a little when he discovered he could blow them up, one galaxy crashing into another and releasing a force equivalent to fifty squillion H-bombs. His son, Jesus, especially liked the blowing up bit, but God was worried he was a little too keen on destruction. He was a big boy now, and really ought to be thinking of doing something *constructive* with his life, not skulking in his room all day. The Holy Spirit wasn't much help either. There had only been the three of them up till now since the beginning of eternity — at least, the ginormous explosion that had kicked the whole thing off all those years ago — but he had never quite figured out what the Holy Ghost actually *did*. He just seemed to waft around looking mysterious.

He was equally puzzled by the appearance of two new companions. He wondered if it was something to do with Jesus. He was painfully aware that his son was streets ahead of him in the technology stakes, and it was Jesus who'd informed him that these two 'archangels', as his son termed them, were called Michael and Gabriel. They seemed to spend a lot of time huddled with Jesus in his room. On the one hand God was pleased that Jesus had some friends close to his own age, but he would like to know where they had come from. He decided to have a word.

II
The Cosmos, Eternity

"Oh, *Dad*," protested Jesus. "I'm busy. And knock before you come in."

The three of them didn't look very busy. They were sat around a big screen — which God had never seen before — which was showing a massive explosion.

"Whoa, dude!" gleefully exclaimed the larger and more stupid looking of the two archangels, Gabriel. "That's so cool! That's Centaurus done for. What next?"

God was being comprehensively ignored. He resolved to put his foot down. His own powers of destruction were a little rusty, but he was able to summon up a reasonably sized thunderbolt, which he directed at the screen. It disappeared in a flash and a bang, and he had the satisfaction of seeing the two archangels actually looking a little shocked.

"Out! Now!"

Even Jesus had been shaken by God's display of anger, and he sheepishly followed his father outside. God led him to the throne room, which was also pretty intimidating, and pointed to the least impressive of the three thrones.

"Sit. There."

Jesus meekly sat down. God decided to defuse the situation.

"Cup of tea?"

He pottered off and returned a couple of minutes later with

two steaming mugs.

"Ah!" breathed God with satisfaction. "The cup that cheers but does not inebriate."

Jesus stayed quiet. He had been experimenting with inebriation, as well as destruction, with his two new friends.

They both silently sipped their tea for a minute or two. Then God said:

"Who are they? Michael and Gabriel? Where did they come from?"

"I dunno," said Jesus. "I thought they were something to do with you."

God sighed. All these mysteries. Maybe the Holy Ghost could shed some light. But they were not the immediate concern. He had been mulling over the idea of creating life. To be sure, he'd let his imagination run riot in some of his creations already, and actually had had a go at creating a sort of lifeform, which hadn't worked out, about half a billion years ago. But he now felt the team needed a real challenge, and he'd really like to create something in their own image — or at least his and Jesus's. It would give Jesus, in particular, something to concentrate on (although he wasn't sure what the Holy Ghost had to contribute) and it could be a lot of fun.

"Son," he said. "It's all a bit out of the box at the moment. But I've got an idea."

Jesus rolled his eyes upwards. He hated it when his father tried hip new language.

They reconvened a couple of days later. God had explained his vision to his son, and, it must be said, was a little disappointed by his reaction. But Jesus had promised to go away and think about it, which was a step forward in itself. God opened the conversation.

"Well, what do you think?"

"There's got to be animals as well."

God was non-plussed.

"What's an animal?"

Jesus was scornful. "Oh, Dad, where have you been? Animals are little furry things. You can't have an ecosystem without animals. Obvs. I thought you were supposed to be all-knowing"

God didn't know what an ecosystem was either, but didn't like to admit to so much ignorance. Things were moving faster than he had intended, but at least his son had been thinking about it, although he suspected the influence of the two archangels. Despite his reservations, he decided on the whole it might be better to delegate some control to his son.

"All right. I'll look after life in my — our — own image, and you can look after the animals or whatever you call them. I'll call mine — oh, I don't know — 'Man'."

"Cool," said Jesus.

III
Croydon, 10th May, 2017

Arthur woke up in his own bed, Jill by his side, feeling wrecked. He groaned, which woke Jill.

"Morning, love," she said. "You had a restless night. And who's Edith?"

Arthur glanced at her sharply. He had a very vivid flashback of what was, for him, the last few weeks, culminating in an entire Anglo-Saxon army on his heels intent on killing him, with Norman archers joining in the fun. For Jill, obviously, it had just been one night. He groaned again. He had no idea what was going on.

Jill was actually getting a little worried by his behaviour. Arthur had always behaved in an abstract kind of way, but recently it was almost as if he was inhabiting another world. She decided to keep a diary of his new eccentricities. The first entry read 'Edith?'

And what of Trevor's feelings in all this? Well, Trevor was a gene, and genes have no opinions or emotions in their own right. Trevor's job was to dump his unwitting host in different epochs at random times and intervals, and he was very good at that job. It was no concern of his what the consequences or ramifications of that dump might be. But Trevor was not God. He was not omnipotent or all knowing. He was just a recessive gene that had got lucky. Twice. In the whole recorded span of history. And one of those was with a mushroom. He could be over-ridden by other bodily functions, like sheer terror. So, when Arthur was fleeing an English army intent on dismembering him, his body flooding with adrenaline, that response took precedence over Trevor, and Arthur was returned unharmed, though highly traumatised, to his own little plot in the space time continuum.

The physics enabling such phenomena as Trevor is pretty blue sky. It is so blue sky that any self-respecting physicist would laugh it out of court. But they laughed at Copernicus. They laughed at Marconi. So up yours, physics. This same blue-sky physics also allows this simultaneous narrative of planetary and biological evolution and a creation myth, and a great deal of elasticity in space/time considerations. Just because you can't get *your* head around it...

IV
The Cosmos, Eternity

"What do you think?" asked God, shyly.

Jesus gazed at the mock-up, which looked remarkably like Michelangelo's statue of David, with one glaring exception.

"He hasn't got a willy," said Jesus.

"He needs a willy," chimed in Michael. The archangels seemed to be proliferating. Michael and Gabriel had been joined by Raphael, Jophiel, Uriel and Azrael. God didn't know where they were coming from, and all they seemed to do was offer up unwanted opinions. He was taken aback by the barrage of criticism.

"What does he need a willy for?" asked God. "I made him in my own image, and I manage perfectly well without one."

Jesus and the archangels tittered amongst themselves. God was flattering himself if he thought he looked like the mock-up, and as for not having a willy, well how hilarious! — even though Jesus and his mates didn't quite know why.

"What have you come up with?" countered God. "Your 'animals'."

Jesus was quite proud of his work. He had not only come up with animals, he had created plants as well. With the help of the archangels, he had organised life into three main groups — the prokaryote, the archaea and the eukaryote, and within each group sub-classified the contents into domains, kingdoms, phyla, classes, orders, families, genuses, species

63

and strains. It had been an all-nighter. There was no doubt that in the whole of creation the kittens were the cuddliest, and that's what he showed to God.

"What's the point of that?" said God, disparagingly.

Jesus was hurt. "What's the point of any of it?" he snapped back.

"Well, my 'Man' will worship me. That's what he's there for. Your 'animals' won't have the intelligence to worship something for which there will be no concrete evidence and which moves in mysterious ways."

Jesus didn't have an immediate answer to that.

The issue of the willy slowed the project down by several millennia. God was quite upset, but Jesus didn't seem to care. He had his band of archangel friends, who seemed to be growing all the time, and he'd gone back to his previous bad habits of blowing up galaxies, and getting up to who knows what with his group of sniggering buddies. But both were essentially in the mood for compromise. God still wanted something to constructively occupy his son, and had distant and, as yet, nebulous plans to actually put Jesus physically into his creation to give him a sense of responsibility. God was also feeling quite lonely. The Holy Ghost, even though he wasn't much of a companion at the best of times, had disappeared completely off the radar, and with the estrangement from Jesus he didn't really have anyone else. Jesus, for his part, had been disappointed not to be able to carry out his creation, particularly the kittens.

And so they came to an agreement. Jesus could have his willy, but it had to have the end chopped off.

"What?" said Jesus, incredulously. "What for?"

But God was adamant. "It's circumcision or nothing," he

decreed.

Jesus realised he was still getting his penis and his kittens, which wasn't a bad outcome after seven thousand four hundred and seven years of mutual sulking.

"OK," he said, gracelessly.

And so, the date of creation — C-Day — was fixed for 6th October, 3761BC.

IV
Croydon, May 2017

Jill thought Arthur was getting better. He had had a couple more restless nights, and she had added the words 'Chad', 'nun' and 'sandals' to her list. He was also starting to open up about what was bothering him. Apparently, he'd had a bad dream about the Battle of Hastings, although she noted he made no further mention of Edith. But Jill was a tolerant lady, and while she trusted Arthur without question, she was fully aware that people did not necessarily have full control over their night time thoughts. Over the years she had heard Arthur mumble 'Nancy' in his sleep, which she knew to be the first name of Mrs. Frobisher from HR, and she herself had had the odd (and wonderful) dream about Idris Elba. She knew he was back to normal when he started banging on about his beermat society.

"Are we doing anything next Friday night?" asked Arthur.

"I don't think so. Why?"

"There's a meeting of the Provisional Wing of the Croydon Beermat Appreciation Society in the George. All welcome, it says. Even wives."

"I'd sooner go to the dentist. The Provisional Wing?"

"Yes, the Provos. Don't ask. They split off from the Officials about three months ago. All egos really. The flashpoint was a pretty nasty row about the authenticity of a 1953 coronation coaster. I went with the Provos."

"Do you have to wear a balaclava to your meetings?"

"Now you're being silly."

Even so, Jill accompanied Arthur to his meeting, and quite enjoyed herself. It was nice to get out.

V
The Cosmos 6th October, 3761BC

An awful lot of effort and organisation had gone into the Creation, and they were pretty well ready to go on the due date. It had been agreed to do it over six days, and have the seventh day off. First up was light. God had decided that given the event would likely go down in posterity, he'd make a bit of a thing about each event. So, he dressed in his best robes, sat on his most impressive throne, and on the dot of H-hour on Day One boomed,

"Let there be light."

There was an immediate problem. Implicit in there being light was that there should be dark as well. Now, whilst God had had the foresight to create the Sun, light and dark were obviously governed by the rotation of the Earth. And the creation of the Earth was not due till Day Three. The watching archangels, of whom there were now hundreds, nudged and tittered amongst themselves, and phrases such as 'piss up in a brewery' and 'bunk up in a brothel' could be distinctly heard amongst the general buzz of conversation.

God hurriedly summonsed Jesus.

"You're responsible for this cock-up."

Jesus was hurt. Neither of them had really thought this one through. There was only one thing for it. God, being omnipotent, decreed that Day One had been successfully concluded, even though it had only lasted ten minutes, and they were now onto Day Two. He resumed his seat on the throne.

"Let there be a firmament in the midst of the waters, and let it divide the waters from the waters."

Nobody really knew what a firmament was, and in the event, it didn't really help, because it turned out that the firmament was Heaven. It was Jesus's turn to be cross.

"Oh, *Dad*," he said. "Couldn't that have waited? In the circumstances?"

Groans were heard from the assembly of angels, and even God had to admit that the creation of Heaven was not urgent. He advanced the clock again. Days One and Two had taken a total of fifteen minutes. He announced the start of Day Three.

"Let the waters under the heaven be gathered unto one place, and let the dry land appear."

This worked quite well, and there was an ironic cheer from the assembled multitude. God felt on a roll, and proceeded with stage two of Day Three.

"Let the earth bring forth grass, the herb yielding seed, and the fruit tree yielding fruit after his kind, whose seed is in itself, upon the earth."

There was a genuine gasp of admiration as a sea of green spread over the land areas of Earth. Jesus hopped up and down with excitement. But Day Three had actually taken all day, and by now God was feeling a bit knackered. He began to regret he'd agreed not to have a day off till Day Seven, and decided they'd had enough pomp and he was just going to get on with it now. His audience was also getting a bit restive and the novelty of creating a brand-new world was wearing off. God turned to Jesus:

"OK, what's next?"

Jesus studied the plans. "Er, lights in the firmament of heaven." He looked around him at the star-studded universe. "We've already got those."

"Let me have a look," said God, and studied the plans himself. "I can only think you blew up one too many galaxies."

"But there's loads."

God looked around himself, and could only agree. He was by now by no means averse to accelerating the process. He wanted to get to the bit where he made 'Man'.

"Day Five, then," said God. These days were bearing less and less relationship to the passage of real time.

"This is where you put my animals on Earth," said Jesus. "Don't forget the kittens!"

God had rather left this bit to Jesus, and was a bit taken aback by the variety of life that suddenly appeared, particularly some nasty slimy things. Jesus's creation seemed to take up an awful lot of space; he hoped there would be room left for his 'Man'.

As it was now the last day, and the whole purpose of God's project was about to be realised, that is, the introduction of 'Man', he decided to make a big thing of it again, despite the fact a lot of the angels and archangels had drifted away. He sat on his throne and proclaimed:

"Let us make Man in our image, after our likeness, and let them have dominion over the fish of the sea, and over the fowl of the air and over the cattle, and over all the Earth, and over every creeping thing that creepeth upon the Earth."

He shot a sly look at Jesus; he hadn't actually cleared this bit with his son. Jesus showed no reaction, however. His creation had gone to plan, and if God — and 'Man' — thought they'd be able to lord it over things like his lions and tigers and rattlesnakes, they would have another think coming.

It was done. Creation was finished. God high fived his son and went off to have a bath.

VI
Heaven, BCE

Creation was not going well. God had anticipated some teething problems, but the way things were going the whole thing was going to fold in on itself. The root cause was 'Man's' messiness. He refused to tidy up after himself, and his rubbish was starting to affect the whole of Earth. Whole species, and a lot of 'Mans' themselves, were dying out from the pollution. The issue was exacerbated by life's inability to replace itself. Whilst God, as a bit of an afterthought on Day Six, had instructed 'Man' to 'be fruitful, and multiply, and replenish the earth', he hadn't actually given 'Man' a means by which to do it. Jesus hadn't really thought about it for his animals either. Another problem, which really paled in comparison to the first one, was that 'Man' was wasting a lot of time playing with his willy. God knew it had been a mistake to give him one.

What to do? He called Jesus for a conflab, and after a bit of toing and froing, they came up with the idea of a companion for 'Man', who would tidy up after him and hopefully be more generally socially responsible. God left the design details to Jesus, the only stipulation being that this one wouldn't have a willy. The prototype would be designated 'Man Mk 2'.

Within a couple of weeks Jesus had come up with his prototype. He had learned from the mistakes of 'Man', and 'Man Mk 2' was smaller, lighter and generally more efficient, and clever than the earlier model. God was happy with the design, and they both thought the prototype was sufficiently different from the original to be named something other than 'Man Mk 2'. It was Jesus who came up with the idea of 'Woman'.

'Woman' was introduced to Creation and was an immediate success. Not only was Creation tidied up, it started to look brighter as 'Woman' insisted that 'Man' did something more constructive with his Saturday afternoons than sitting around watching footie and drinking beer. Things called 'shops' started appearing, and a new craze of 'cooking' swept the earth. God was well pleased with developments.

But he still hadn't cracked the 'be fruitful' bit.

VII
Heaven, BCE

One minute Arthur was in the little kitchen at work making a cup of tea, the next he was amongst a throng of heavenly angels. He rubbed his eyes. Was he dead? He had been a bit worried about the kettle at work — it had taken out all the electrics in the building on more than one occasion. Had it had its revenge on Arthur for reporting it to the maintenance team? But with a queasy feeling in the pit of his stomach he guessed this might be a rerun of his previous experience with King Harold and Edith.

He gazed apprehensively around him. He was surrounded by angels all right. Beautiful blond-haired beings with bright haloes clad in flowing white robes edged in gold, wings tucked neatly behind their backs. But the atmosphere was not one of joyful praise to God, more of a rowdy all male boarding school on Founders Day. They seemed to be in some kind of dining hall, the angels seated at twenty-five or more long communal tables. There was a central raised dais, where a dozen more angels sat. Their behaviour appeared altogether more responsible than that of their fellows at the long tables, and Arthur surmised they might be the more senior. He was right; it was the archangels who had the privilege of occupying the central dais. The walls of the hall were adorned with Italianate looking paintings of plump cherubs fluttering around nubile semi-clad maidens and reclining males with a striking resemblance to Michelangelo's David reaching out to nervous looking acolytes.

Bursts of song floated up from the benches, but not, as Arthur expected, hymns of praise glorifying the deity. He caught snatches of 'Ah-hum, titty bum, titty bum, titty bum, an engineer told me before he died, Ah-hum, ah-hum...' and 'Dinah, Dinah, show us your leg, show us your leg...' The occasional bread roll flew through the air, accompanied by gusts of raucous laughter. There was also a strong smell of spilt beer.

The angel sitting next to Arthur turned to him, and looked him up and down in a friendly way.

"Hello. You're new, aren't you? I like your get-up — very original. I'm Afriel."

Arthur began to relax. It didn't seem like he was going to face an immediate hanging.

"I'm Arthur," he replied. "Where am I?"

Afriel looked at him with fond amusement. "You're in Heaven, silly."

Arthur digested that fact. Maybe he had died. But this was nothing like the heaven he'd been told about.

"Am I dead?" he asked.

It was Afriel's turn to look puzzled. "What's dead?"

Arthur decided to go with the flow. "Is this how you spend your days?"

"No!" said Afriel. "This is just dinner. We go partying after this. And then we go to bed, then it's time for dinner again."

"What about God? I thought angels spent all day praising him."

Afriel giggled. "He's an old dear, but we let him get on with it, and he lets us get on with it. It's fun! Come and meet my friends."

VIII
Heaven, BCE

The 'be fruitful' thing was proving to be a problem. The idea was sound enough — that man should be self-replenishing — but it just wasn't happening. The earth was reasonably well stocked for the moment, although God wasn't clear where all the other 'Mans' and 'Womans' had come from. He put these conundrums to one side and summonsed Jesus for an emergency meeting.

"Hello, Dad," said Jesus. "Is it a quick one?" He'd been pulled away from the angels, with whom he now spent most of his waking (and sleeping) hours.

"I won't keep you from your day job for long," said God, with a hint of sarcasm. "But we have to get 'Man' sorted. We have to get him to reproduce."

"Can't you do it?" asked Jesus. He assumed that God had created all man (and woman) kind. God had not wanted to admit he had no idea where all the others, apart from the original prototypes, had come from.

"It's not my job to keep the human race going," he huffed. "They're supposed to be self-sufficient."

They both gazed down at Creation.

"The grass seems to be doing pretty well," observed Jesus. "And the herb yielding seed and fruit-tree bearing fruit."

It was true. Despite 'Man's' best efforts to destroy his habitat, vegetation was thriving.

"How do they do it?" asked God.

"They bud," replied Jesus.

"Bingo!" exclaimed God.

They decided to be democratic about the whole thing, and invited the two prototypes (who now, by the way, had adopted the names 'Adam' and 'Eve') back up to Heaven for their views. The plan was that the 'Woman' should do the budding because, while there was no doubt the introduction of 'Woman' had been good for Creation as a whole, both God and Jesus agreed that housekeeping, cooking, cleaning, ironing, fetching and carrying still left 'Woman' plenty of time for other duties. Adam had no problem with this.

They explained the plan to Eve, and showed her how plants and micro-organisms reproduced by budding. Eve was not impressed.

"Where are they going to come from?" she demanded. "And how am I going to be able to do things if I've got a big hairy thing hanging off me? Or more than one? Why can't I just have a baby?"

It must be said God and Jesus hadn't really thought this through. They simply assumed that 'Woman' would be able to cope like they usually did. But they weren't prepared to give up on the idea.

After a lot of haggling a compromise was achieved. There would only be one bud at a time, it would develop under the arm, and it would drop off when it was the size of a baby. 'Man' would be expected to help with the housework when 'Woman' was budding, and would provide flowers on at least a weekly basis.

Fruitfulness was sorted.

IX
Heaven, BCE

Arthur was having a jolly good time. He had now spent a couple of days (and nights) carousing in the company of Afriel and his best friends, Azazel, Azza and Uzza, and the unofficial leader of the group, Shemyaza. He had been introduced to a variety of intoxicating, and even narcotic, substances, and now understood why their days consisted only of carousing, sleeping and eating. But despite the almost continuous partying, accompanied by the singing of the bawdiest of songs, there was a curious innocence about the whole thing. There was no talk of sexual adventure, which is almost axiomatic amongst groups of merry-making young men (Arthur assumed they *were* young men). After a particularly indecent verse of The Engineer's Song — 'in and out went the prick of steel, and round and round went the bloody great wheel...' — Arthur turned to Afriel and said, curiously but cautiously,

"You do understand what that's all about?"

"Of course I do, silly! It's about a man who makes a funny machine," Afriel replied, gaily.

"What about 'Dinah, Dinah, show us your leg — a yard above the knee'?"

"You don't have to analyse them," exclaimed Afriel. "They're just funny songs!"

Shemyaza had been listening in to this conversation with great interest.

"Do you think there's more to them, then?" he asked Arthur.

Arthur felt put on the spot. He was no prude, but was it his place to educate his new friends in the facts of life? If indeed these facts applied in the current circumstances. But, fuelled by a particularly potent pint of mead, he decided it couldn't do any harm.

Indeed, it didn't, and mankind should be eternally grateful for Arthur's decision. But it caused a bit of a kerfuffle in Heaven.

X
Heaven, BCE

"What?" screamed God.

God had quite naturally taken an ongoing and fatherly interest in developments in his Creation, particularly how some of the resolutions to the problems they'd encountered were going on. He was gratified to see there was a baby boom, which kept the 'Womans', in particular, very happy. However closely he looked, though, he couldn't see very much budding going on. He had noticed that sometimes the 'Womans' got very fat, then very quickly regained their original figures. He sent his most trusted archangel, Raphael, down to investigate, and now the angel was reporting back.

"What?" screamed God again. Jesus had joined the pair, and even he looked pale at Raphael's news.

"Well, sir, it appears that the 'Mans' and 'Womans' are having sex."

"What's sex?"

"Er, it's when a 'Man' and a 'Woman' get very close, and then there's a baby."

"Does it involve willies?" asked God, suspiciously.

"Er, to the best of my knowledge, yes, sir, it does."

God glared at Jesus. "I said willies were a mistake." Jesus shuffled his feet uncomfortably. He turned back to Raphael. "And where did they pick up this filthy habit from?"

It was Raphael's turn to shift awkwardly.

"It seems to be the angels, or at least some of them. The ring leader was Shemyaza. They descended to earth and — er — seduced anyone they took a fancy to. And the 'Mans' and 'Womans' down there decided they preferred it."

God went ballistic.

"Sort it out!" he screeched at Raphael.

And so it came to pass that Raphael couldn't sort it out, because man-kind (and a lot of animal-kind) were not prepared to give up this novel and fun way of making babies. God had a sort of revenge, though, because for ever after it was associated with guilt and wickedness and all sorts of other contradictions. As for Shemyaza, Afriel and all their straying angelic friends, they were expelled from Heaven, and joined up with another fallen angel, Satanail, to write a whole new chapter in theology.

All thanks to Arthur.

Per Ardua

I
Huntsville, Alabama, 1st July, 1960

The two Americans sat sipping their beers in the downtown bar.

"So, Wernher got the job then," said Ted, the older and larger of the two men.

"Yeah," said Al, ruminatively.

They were both colonels in the United States Air Force, experts in rocketry, and had been seconded to the newly established George C. Marshall Space Flight Center in Huntsville, Alabama. The two men had known each other since being based at the same airfield in England during the dying days of the Second World War, and were good friends.

"Think we can trust him? Wernher?"

Al paused before answering. "Well, he hates the Reds as much as we do. More even."

The subject of discussion was Wernher von Braun, the ex-Technical Director of the German rocket programme, purloined, together with his team of German rocket engineers, after the defeat of Nazi Germany in 1945, and since then the backbone of the American space effort. The Russians had helped themselves to another wodge of German scientists, and it seemed like the Russians' Germans were doing rather better than the Americans'. After a string of humiliating defeats in the space race with the Soviet Union, President Eisenhower had established the National Aeronautics and Space Administration (NASA) based at Huntsville, with von Braun at its helm.

"Who else does he hate, though?" asked Ted.

"You mean...?"

"What I mean," continued Ted, "Is that a couple of years back, at the start of the Redstone program, I analysed one of his Kraut's flight plans for the prototype ballistic missile. Do you know where it was targeted?"

"Tell me," said Al.

"London. London, England. If we'd gone ahead with the firing, we'd have taken out the capital of our nearest and dearest ally."

"Not so near and dear at the moment," replied Al. "They seem cock a hoop the Reds are beating us hands down."

"Even so, Ike would have had some difficulty explaining it away. Especially as it was going out live on TV."

"You managed to save our diplomatic relations with the Brits, though. Obviously."

"A couple of tweaks and it just fell into the Atlantic. The Krauts weren't too pleased. Couldn't say anything, though, but I've kept a very careful eye on them since."

"I can imagine," said Al.

II
Croydon, May 2017

Jill was aware that Arthur had had another episode, and had added the words 'Shemyaza', 'engineer' and 'mead' to her list. Whatever Arthur had been through this time did not seem to be as traumatic as previously, though. Indeed, she had caught him humming snatches of songs that took her back to a dim and distant pre-Arthur past, a time when fun was an integral part of life, particularly the boisterous rugby crowd she spent her early university career with. She brushed away a nostalgic tear.

Life had very much returned to normal, that is until two Mormons appeared on the doorstep. Like much of the rest of the population Jill and Arthur dismissed them as politely and as soon as possible, but on this occasion Arthur — and it was Arthur that had opened the door to them — seemed to be relishing the conversation. He also seemed to be remarkably well informed, which further puzzled Jill. Along with everything else, apart from beermats, Arthur had taken no apparent interest in religion. It was now the Mormons who were itching to get away after being pinned for half an hour on the doorstep, during which she distinctly heard the word 'Shemyaza' mentioned. Arthur's assertion that 'he had never come across your angel Moroni' finally terminated the conversation as the Mormons took offence and stalked off.

Later, she quietly googled 'Shemyaza', to discover he was

the leader of the fallen angels of biblical tradition. Where on earth had Arthur picked up an interest in Old Testament theology?

III
The Oval Office, 22nd May, 1961

President Kennedy was on the phone.

"Of course I love ya, baby... Yeah, I've never had such a good time... Course we gotta do it again... Sometime... Yeah, soon, very soon... Yeah, I really love the way you do that — thing. No, you know I can't take you to the movies... I know you're in this new movie... Yeah, I'll go and see it... No, you know I gotta take Jackie..."

There was a loud knock on the door.

"Marilyn... I gotta go... No really, I gotta go... LBJ's here... Marilyn, don't... Oh!"

Lyndon Baines Johnson strode into the Office, a broad smirk on his face.

"Not interrupting anything, Jack? Am I?"

Kennedy shuffled uncomfortably in his chair.

"Lyndon. Yo! How ya doing? What have you got to tell me? About getting to the moon?"

The US administration was in a bit of a panic. A month or so ago, the Russians had successfully sent a man into space. And had got him back again. Also, the previous month had seen the failed Bay of Pigs invasion of Cuba, when an invasion force of exiles, backed by the full might of the US military, had been routed by the ragtag forces of Fidel Castro. President Kennedy needed some good PR, and, despite having previously viewed the whole space thing as the preserve of overgrown schoolboys, dubious ex-Nazis and a complete waste of money, had despatched his Vice President on a mission to investigate the feasibility of putting an American on the moon. Preferably by the end of the month.

"Good news and bad news, Jack."

Kennedy groaned. "Let's start with the bad news."

"The Krauts don't think they can even hit the moon yet, let alone land someone on it. And get them back. They think it'll take about ten years."

"Christ alive! Ten years! It's fucking big enough. What's their problem? They didn't seem to have any problem hitting London, and that's a lot smaller than the moon. That's very un-American."

"That's because they're Krauts," responded Johnson, reasonably.

"OK, OK. What's the good news?"

"They think it'll take the Reds ten years as well. So we gotta chance of getting even."

"Oh, brilliant. Where are you and me gonna be in ten years? I need something now."

"It's not gonna do either of us any good if you start shooting your fellow Americans at the moon and they miss, or splat onto the surface. Look, we'll tell the Krauts there's a deadline of the end of the sixties, and we'll call it something classy, get the public on board. I know — when's Marilyn's birthday?"

"Can we not talk about Marilyn? Please?"

"C'mon. This'll make her really happy. And keep her off your back. And nobody will make the connection."

"June 1st."

"Great. We'll call it Gemini!"

IV
Croydon, May 2017

Jill was a year or so younger than Arthur, and they had been together since the end of her second year at university. Whilst her relationship with Arthur had represented an abrupt change of gear in her lifestyle, she felt it was all part of growing up and had had few regrets. Up until now. Well, maybe regret was too strong a word for what she was feeling. It was Arthur's humming of snatches of rugby songs that had triggered her nostalgia. Had her then lifestyle been all that bad? In the long run? She had not really kept in touch with any of her pre-Arthur crowd, particularly her unreliable boyfriend, but she was aware most of them had not done badly. One was now a Professor of Biology at, admittedly, a not very prestigious university, and her ex-boyfriend had established a highly successful chain of estate agents.

She burrowed into the depths of her wardrobe and pulled out a dusty photo album. It covered her final couple of years at school and her time as an undergraduate at the University of Newport Pagnell. She gazed at the photos of herself. A pretty, petite, fair haired girl returned her gaze. She sighed, and carried on flicking through the album. The final pages had some pictures of Arthur. He *was* quite cute, she reflected, with something of the Jeremy Irons about him, and she again told herself that with her final year approaching her all night clubbing had had to be curtailed, and Arthur was certainly the man to help her do that. But did their life after university have to be quite so predictable and Croydon centric?

She flicked back to the front of the album. There were the pictures of her first-year summer vacation trip to Greece, when she and her friends had lived in an olive grove on Crete. Gosh! She'd never realised it before but in one photo she was topless, albeit in the distance. She giggled and blushed, and turned more pages. She paused on a picture of her and her gang emerging from a nightclub at dawn, her arm wrapped around her ex-boyfriend, Chris. She studied it, trying to name the half dozen or so figures in the foreground, and then noticed the date underneath the picture. It said May 1985. She looked again. It couldn't have been. She was with Arthur by then.

V
The Premier's Office, The Kremlin, 10th June, 1961

"Yo, Leonid!"

Leonid Brezhnev lowered his considerable bulk into the chair facing his leader's desk.

"Pardon, Comrade Khrushchev?"

"'Yo!' It's what all the Americans say to each other. And 'fuck'. They say 'fuck' a lot."

"You enjoyed your trip to Vienna then, comrade?" said Brezhnev with a heavy hint of sarcasm.

Nikita Khrushchev, leader of the USSR, had just returned from a summit in Vienna, where he had met and negotiated with the American president, Jack Kennedy. Although the summit had been a failure, Khrushchev, already enchanted with all things American since his visit to the USA in 1959, had been smitten by the charismatic new president.

"He knows Marilyn Monroe!" he enthused. "Why don't we have any beautiful women? All we have is beefy female athletes."

"The Press sisters are women," Brezhnev reminded his boss. "We can't have any suggestion they're not."

The Press sisters, Tamara and Irina, were world beating Soviet athletes, Tamara in shot put and discus, and Irina on the track. There was some speculation about their actual sex.

"I hear the Olympic Committee are going to be exploring

the contents of athletes' underpants before the next Games," sneered Khrushchev. "Not personally, of course."

"They must have got the idea from Kennedy and Marilyn Monroe."

Khrushchev was genuinely shocked. Marilyn Monroe was one of the American icons he revered, along with self-service cafeterias and Disneyland.

"Where did you hear that?"

Brezhnev sighed. His boss's infatuation with the USA was not doing him any favours amongst the hatchet-faced men of the Politburo, Brezhnev included.

"Comrade, I didn't come here today to discuss whether or not President Kennedy is shagging Marilyn Monroe. Our meeting is to discuss our progress in space and the American response. What did you learn from Kennedy?"

Khrushchev reluctantly dragged himself away from his mental vision of Kennedy and Marilyn exploring each other's underpants.

"They're pretty pissed off, as you can imagine. They sent someone up a couple of days after Yuri got back, but all he did was go up and come back down again, not orbit like our lad. And he wasn't as good looking as Yuri. The whole world think we've got one up on them, even the Brits."

"The British hate the Americans more than they hate us," said Brezhnev. "They never forgave them for winning their war for them. And stealing their women."

"Our women were pretty safe," muttered Khrushchev.

Brezhnev chose to ignore the remark. "And the American response?"

"Brace yourself. They want to collaborate putting a man on the moon."

Brezhnev was taken aback. "That would mean allowing them access to our programs. They'd realise our missiles would barely reach Poland, let alone Washington. And our spacecraft are like tin cans compared to theirs."

"That's being unfair to tin cans," replied Khrushchev.

"We can't possibly do it. We'll get one of ours up there first. However."

"Weeell," said Khrushchev, his mind whirling with visions of VIP trips to Cape Canaveral, Disneyland and Marilyn Monroe. "I don't know."

VI
Croydon, May 2017

Arthur and Jill had two cats, Mish and Mash, Burmese and brothers. Mish was the brains of the partnership, while Mash, while not entirely stupid, provided the brawn. Mash would unmercifully bully Mish at times, but Mish could out psych Mash by simply staring at him. Mish was, in fact, a little bit fey.

Like most cats they regarded their keepers as two not very competent servants.

"My God," Mash would say to Mish. "It's not rocket science. All they have to do is provide regular food, a fresh litter tray, and warmth. And not close doors." Mash had a fundamental objection to closed doors and did not mind the world knowing about it. His biggest problem was the downstairs toilet. Whenever anyone went in there, particularly Jill, Mash would pace anxiously outside yelling. It was not just the closed door in this instance; he was panic stricken the occupant would never emerge.

Mish generally let him ramble on. If he was moaning about the servants, he wasn't beating Mish up. But on this occasion, he joined in.

"Something's up," he said.

Cats have had a chequered history with humans. They first realised the benefits of owning humans about one hundred thousand years ago, and for most of the time since have enjoyed an exploitative relationship, humans, of course, thinking it was the other way around. But their sixth sense, if you like, was rumbled in the Middle Ages, when the Catholic Church officially declared them agents of Satan, and organised the destruction of as many as possible. The cats had their revenge, though, when the proliferation of rats and mice due the shortage of cats was a major factor in the spread of the Black Death. Up yours, was the collective feline view. Cats were rehabilitated by no one less than Queen Victoria, and the Victorians adopted them wholesale, enchanted by their cuddliness. That was also a mistake.

"What do you mean, something's up?" asked Mash, annoyed to be distracted from his favourite rant.

"The black and white one." The cats distinguished Arthur and Jill by the usual colour of their clothing. Whilst cats did not waste too much time thinking about humankind, they were endemically puzzled by the way humans changed the colour of their fur on a daily basis. They were also alert to any change that might affect their own wellbeing. "He's away with the fairies."

Mash's ears pricked up. He may have generally used his brother as a punchbag, but he had considerable respect for Mish's sensory powers. And for him to interrupt Mash in full flow it must be something important. "Go on," he said.

Mish paused to wash his bum. "He goes away. To strange places. And when he comes back, he doesn't know he's gone. But it's getting worse. He might go altogether."

The cats considered the implications of this. If Arthur disappeared, they might have to train someone else. And that would take effort.

"The colourful one needs to know," said Mash.

The sixth sense of cats was effectively telepathy. They did not generally waste this aptitude on humans, deeming them too unimportant. But this situation might affect their welfare.

"I'll sort it," said Mish.

VII
Washington DC, June 1965

A lot had happened in the last couple of years. LBJ was now in the White House after the murder of JFK in 1963. In late 1964 in the Soviet Union Khrushchev had been ousted by Leonid Brezhnev, and to most people's relief if hadn't involved the use of an ice pick. The Russians' Germans were still a nose ahead of the Americans' Germans in the space race, but the latter were closing the gap. Also, the world had nearly ended as a result of the Cuban missile crisis in October 1962. At this juncture in history LBJ had thought it expedient to invite Brezhnev to Washington, partly to defuse a still twitchy international situation, but also because he wanted to be seen to have, if not friends, at least 'special relationships'. Jack Kennedy had had lots of 'special relationships', and not just with Hollywood starlets. Britain's Harold MacMillan and Kennedy had had an almost father/son relationship, and Khrushchev had obviously worshipped Kennedy, even though he tried to blow him up in 1962. Kennedy returned that affection as one might to an old and smelly dog. LBJ was not getting on with the UK's new premier, Harold Wilson, who was refusing to send British troops to murder innocent civilians in Vietnam, which really only left Brezhnev, as obviously neither Mao Zedong nor General De Gaulle, the only other two likely candidates as world leaders, would be up for a couple of beers and a Texas barbeque brisket. Being

Russian, Brezhnev would obviously like a drink, but Johnson was nervous about how they might otherwise get on. He knew Kennedy had dangled the idea of co-operation in getting to the moon, and that might be way to go. Any other global compromise could just be too scary.

Brezhnev was also anxious about the visit. He did not have the gregarious temperament of his predecessor, and was conscious that too close a relationship with the Americans would expose his own country's lack of sophistication in pretty well every sphere going. On the other hand, he was also aware that the USA and Russia could blow each other up several times over, with plenty to spare for the rest of the world, and that some kind of co-operation, or détente, was absolutely necessary. He had independently arrived at the conclusion the space race might be the way to do it.

The meeting did not go well. Brezhnev was, well, just too Russian, and Johnson too Texan. A glimmer of co-operation emerged on the race to the moon, however. Nothing like a full-blown joint effort — Brezhnev was still too conscious of his own country's deficiencies in refinement, and Johnson had a bout of nerves about what his fellow Texans might call collaboration with a commie. What they did agree was to keep each other updated on each other's progress. It was fed to the press as the greatest meeting of minds ever.

The immediate problem that Johnson had was there was no progress to report; in fact, the Soviets still seemed streets ahead in their achievements. Regular reports were arriving from the USSR detailing their latest triumphs, while nothing was going the other way. Johnson was getting desperate.

And then chaos theory, in the shape of the Butterfly Effect, intervened. Princess Margaret, renegade sister of

Queen Elizabeth II of England, was on a wild, but private, tour of the West Coast of the US, spending much of her time enjoying Hollywood hospitality to the full. The British government, desperate for cash from anywhere, persuaded her to turn it into a semi-official visit in order to charm the Americans. When they finished up in Washington, Johnson, still in search of a 'special relationship', invited her to a reception at the White House. The function, and the tour as a whole, gained such notoriety that Margaret was not trusted with an American tour for a very long time. But during the course of the evening Margaret told Johnson of a brilliant screenwriter she'd met in Hollywood, who was promoting a highly realistic series of space adventures. Johnson's ears pricked up. The Russians obviously had difficulty in distinguishing fact from fantasy. Perhaps they could be fed episodes of this space fantasy as evidence of American progress.

And so, the Soviet Embassy was informed that a new documentary series on American achievements in space would be airing soon on TV. It was to be called 'Star Trek'.

VIII
Croydon, May 2017

Jill was a pretty grounded person, and being a career civil servant, although in a different department from Arthur, dealt in facts and evidence. Despite her job, she did have a fairly healthy scepticism about what the government sometimes came out with. Less healthily, perhaps, she also had a bit of a weakness for internet conspiracy theories. She told herself that these ideas were just a bit of fun, but in, admittedly occasional, earnest conversations with friends and family about the burning issues of the day, her fellow participants sometimes thought the ideas surfaced a little too often. Putting a kind interpretation on this, Jill was a little more open to off the wall concepts than might otherwise be imagined, or deemed wise.

And so it was that, on the Tube to work one morning, the thought suddenly flashed through her mind that Arthur was time travelling. Any other person might have instantly dismissed and forgotten the thought, but Jill could not put the idea to one side. Fantastic though it was, the apparent reality of Arthur's recent medieval and theological experiences, together with that confusingly dated photograph, could indicate something very odd indeed was going on.

Job done, thought Mish with quiet satisfaction.

Arthur, now the only member of his household not to have knowledge or suspicion of his time travel, was enjoying the return to his normal life, and his recent experiences were fading in his memory. He, like Jill, was not prone to introspection, and if he thought about his historic adventures at all, it was only a faint yearning for Edith, who had for the moment supplanted Mrs. Frobisher as the object of his extra marital fantasies. He'd resumed his normal route to work, that is, walking from Charing Cross to Smith Square when the weather was fine, and his fear of being apprehended for treason by two heavily armed Anglo-Saxon soldiers had almost entirely disappeared. He had also, call it a midlife crisis if you will, taken to going out for the occasional lunch to a local sandwich bar.

He was later to recall that it was a Thursday, yes, definitely a Thursday in late May, that he found himself sitting opposite two very senior looking American officers. That, of itself, was not remarkable. What was, was that his scruffy little sandwich bar had transformed itself into an American diner.

IX
Titusville. Fl, May 1969

Ted and Al were now very senior US Air Force officers, and had been deeply involved in the American space programme since 1960. They were grabbing a swift lunch in a downtown diner in Titusville, Florida, just over the water from Cape Kennedy, and Ted was worried.

"But I thought Apollo 10 went well?" queried Al. Apollo 10 was the final dress rehearsal for the moon landing that was due to be carried out by Apollo 11 a mere two months later in July.

"Yeah, it got to the moon, did a couple of circuits, got as close as fifty thousand feet in fact, everything looking hunky dory, but when it tried to simulate release of the lunar module, all the computers just fried. Went bang. There just wasn't enough computing power to get the module safely down. Let alone get it back up again."

"And we have to go in July?"

"Reds are nearly there, apparently."

"Do we have any backup?" asked Al, pragmatically.

Ted lowered his voice. "This is top secret. Really top secret. The brass is negotiating with Hollywood to build a set looking like the moon and fake the whole thing. Put it out as the real deal."

Arthur appeared in the booth opposite them. Ted did a double take before his face contorted in horror.

"Jesus Christ!" he screamed. "Where did you come from?"

Al desperately tried to hush him. "Ted, the whole fuckin' restaurant can hear you!"

With great effort Ted managed to calm his voice. "Who the fuck are you?" he hissed at Arthur. "How much have you heard?"

Arthur, in fact, had not heard very much at all. He was too horrified by the turn of events in his own situation. He stared aghast at the two livid and frightened Americans. Through his dismay understanding dawned that he was, yet again, in a seriously compromising situation. He glanced anxiously around. There were, at least, no nuns dangling from the rafters. He returned his gaze to Ted and Al.

"I'm, er, Arthur. Arthur Smith. Civil servant. British."

Ted and Al hadn't reached the upper echelons of the US military without good reason, and they now moved to calm their own panic and regain control of the situation.

"Where the fuck did you come from? And how much did you hear?" Ted repeated.

Arthur himself was beginning to calm down. Americans didn't summarily execute people. Unless they were Vietnamese.

"I didn't hear anything. Really. And I have no idea how I got here. Except it's happened before."

"Happened before?"

Arthur quite rightly felt that any detailed explanations would not necessarily help.

"It's a long story," he said, miserably.

An hour later Arthur found himself in a military police, holding cell.

X
Titusville. Fl, May 1969

Arthur was left to stew for several hours. His mind had gone numb. He had no conceivable strategy to cope with his new situation, and his previous experiences with Edith and Afriel offered no guide for coping with his current predicament. He did have a small window though, through which there was a distant view of what appeared to be a space complex. He had actually been to Florida when the kids were teenagers, and it gradually dawned on him that he was looking out at Cape Canaveral. He could also now recall the odd word caught from Ted before he went ballistic — 'moon', 'fake' and 'Hollywood'. One of Jill's favourite conspiracy theories had been that the 1969 moon landing had been faked in a Hollywood studio. He had landed in the final stages of the American moon-shot in 1969.

Ted came to see Arthur around five o'clock in the afternoon. He had calmed down, and whilst Arthur's sudden appearance had no doubt been a total shock, he and Al had reassured each other there could have been no possible breach of security, especially now Arthur was safely contained. Arthur was very glad to see him, and had decided to be as upfront and honest as possible.

He found a receptive audience in Ted. There was a branch of the US military that Ted had briefly been involved with that was charged with investigating what most sane people would regard as barking mad theories — UFOs, the actual sex of Tamara and Irina Press, whether the Earth really was flat — and time travel was one of them. Ted had thought that had rather more legs than the other stuff.

"So, where — and when — are you from?" he asked.

"Croydon, near London. Summer 2017."

Ted had amazingly heard of Croydon because of the pre-war aerodrome.

"2017," he mused, and then geared himself up for the sixty-four-thousand-dollar question. "Do we get to the moon? On time? For real?"

Arthur briefly found himself in an ethical quandary. Should he be telling this American some very pertinent facts about his near future? It had been OK telling Edith about aeroplanes and democracy and mobile phones because he knew Edith really didn't have a clue what he was talking about. 'Sod it', thought Arthur. 'In for a penny…'

"Yes," he said.

Ted's face split into a broad smile, and he heaved a sigh of relief. It was now Ted's turn to be open.

"We have issues," he said. "With the computers. How do we beat it?"

Arthur had reached the limit of his helpfulness. He knew it was an absolute miracle that the space programme had ever happened given the relatively primitive computers of the sixties, but they were a mystery to him. He shrugged helplessly. Ted's face fell.

"But we do get there? In July?"

"You do. July 20th, 1969."

Ted blanched again. The landing date was another top secret. Who *was* this Limey?

Arthur had had his pockets emptied upon his detention. He didn't carry much, but now Ted plonked his wallet and mobile phone on the table between them. The wallet's function was self-evident, but Ted was curious about the phone. He turned over and about in his hand.

"What's this?" he asked.

"It's my phone," Arthur replied. "But it won't work here. There's no signal and no internet."

"What the fuck's internet?"

Arthur reprised the conversation he had had with Edith, although with a touch more technical detail and rather less flirtation. Within the Settings option he was able to demonstrate some of the phone's specifications.

"That's the RAM value," he said, hoping that Ted wouldn't ask what RAM was. "2.5 GB, it says."

Now, Ted actually did know a thing or two about computers. "Jesus wept," he exclaimed. "Apollo's is a millionth of that. What's this CPU?"

"That's the Central Processing Unit," he said, proudly. Having until recently had no idea what a CPU was, and discovering his ignorance in tête-à-tête with Edith, he had looked it up on Wikipedia. "Mine's 2.5 GHz."

"Christ! That's a hundred thousand times faster."

Ted's brain whirred and clicked. He now had a lead on meeting the moon-shot deadline.

"You — and it — are coming with me."

XI
Huntsville, Alabama, June – July 1969

The next few weeks passed in a whirl for Arthur. His status had transitioned from military detainee to VIP. The evening of his release from detention he had been flown with Ted by military helicopter, Wagner's Ride of the Valkyries running through his head, to Huntsville to meet up with the research teams planning and preparing the moon-shot. Of course, the object of interest was his phone rather than Arthur himself, but while he could claim very little knowledge of how the thing actually worked, the techies were deeply interested in what the phone was capable of. Arthur's bashful descriptions of online pornography were a particular hit. The upshot was that the research teams were able to incorporate Arthur's phone into the Lunar Module, and the vastly increased computer power not only gave it the ability to land and take off safely, but carry out aerial acrobatics should the crew so choose. Which they didn't.

The moon landing was a global and seminal event, watched live by hundreds of millions, including Arthur from the NASA control room itself. He was amongst the wildly cheering ground staff as Neil Armstrong uttered the first human words to come from the surface of the moon:

"Fuck me, I've tripped."

Luckily, the time lag in communications enabled this to be discreetly edited out.

Arthur woke Jill with his cheering and yelling.

"Another dream, dear?" she asked in concern.

Arthur wasn't sure. Strange thing was, later that day, he couldn't find his phone.

America, America

I
The Court of Ferdinand and Isabella of Spain, January 1492

Christopher Columbus was making a superhuman effort to control his irritation.

"Your Majesty, it is accepted by all men of learning, going back as far as the ancient Greeks, that the earth is round. So if you, in your graciousness and generosity, would support my expedition to find a western passage to Cathay, the ships would not, I can categorically state, would not fall off the edge of the Earth."

"Piffle," replied Queen Isabella, haughtily. "Holy Mother Church is adamant that the Earth is flat, and I would be wasting my money on your ridiculous schemes. And are those the same Greeks that enjoyed interfering with little boys? And goats?"

"I'm not aware of any accusations about goats, ma'am," Columbus replied, stiffly. "But the father of modern astronomy, Ptolemy…"

"He sounds Egyptian," interrupted Isabella. "We've just got rid of that lot."

Isabella and her husband, Ferdinand II of Aragon, had recently cleared Granada of the Islamic Moors, their last stronghold in Spain, and she was in no mood to be lectured about eminent North African scientists.

"We would know nothing about the Earth and astronomy," Columbus struggled on, "If it wasn't…"

Isabella cut in again. "Well, I for one don't believe in all that nonsense. 'What are you? Taurus? You'll meet a tall dark stranger. And you, Aquarius? You'll meet a tall dark stranger too'." She smirked and nudged her husband, delighted by her own wit. Ferdinand rolled his eyes heavenwards.

"Ptolemy is the father of astronomy, not astrology," Columbus replied, weakly. He realised he was fighting a losing battle.

Christopher Columbus had had a bee in his bonnet about a western route to the fabulously wealthy Far East since the early 1480s, and had first attempted to raise financial support for an expedition in 1485. But he had been rejected by pretty well every court in Europe, who either shared Queen Isabella's concern that he would just fall off the edge of the Earth, or while accepting that the Earth was round were highly dubious of his claims that it would be a piece of cake (in fairness, Columbus, though right in principle, had very considerably under-estimated how far it was and how long it would take). So, trying to get the rulers of Spain on board was really the last throw of the dice, and it looked like it had failed.

"It is time for our royal lunch," announced Isabella. She liked her tapas bang on the stroke of midday. "Good day!"

Columbus disconsolately rode his hire mule out of town, his dreams finally shattered.

But there was a glimmer of hope.

"Izzy," said Ferdinand to his wife over lunch. "Aren't we being a little bit hasty?"

"Mmmm! Try these albondigas," she replied. "They're yummy."

109

Ferdinand tried again. "All these wars we've had have cost an arm and a leg."

"Money! It's all you ever go on about. You even cancelled that lovely little castle I wanted built on the Costas."

"That could go towards funding this Columbus chappy. If he's right, it could give us a monopoly on a quick new route to the Orient." He decided to apply a touch of psychology. "Think of all those silks and spices flowing through Spain. You'd have first pick."

Isabella's ears visibly pricked up. "Now you put it that way…"

And so Columbus got his funding.

II
Croydon, May 2017

"Jill! Jill, have you seen my phone?" cried Arthur, plaintively. "I can't find it."

"Where did you last have it?" she replied, pragmatically.

Arthur was suddenly nonplussed. Where did he last have it? Yesterday evening, in his inside jacket pocket, where he always kept it? Or was it when he handed it to Ted, in his detention cell in Titusville. His dreams were becoming horribly realistic. 'Aye, aye,' thought Mish.

"Who shut that bloody door?" yelled Mash.

"I think Mash wants to go out," said Jill.

'Servants!' thought Mash.

"Have you found your phone?" asked Jill.

Arthur did not reply, which Jill put down to his having found his phone in some blindingly obvious place. At that point she had made no connection between the missing phone and Arthur's latest dream, but she had added the words 'Apollo', 'CPU' and 'Titusville' to her list. She had also been doing some internet searches on time travel. Starting off at the respectable end of the spectrum (well, Wikipedia), she'd learnt that conceptualising backwards time travel was to all intents and purposes impossible, unless you were a physicist with a brain the size of a small planet. Forwards time travel, on the other hand, seemed a piece of cake. Thing was, all Arthur's adventures seemed to have been in the past, so she was no further forward. Temporarily thwarted, and Jill being Jill, she turned to some conspiracy theories, and became quite indignant that nearly all of them had been debunked. Why shouldn't that photo of someone holding a mobile phone on a beach in Newquay in 1943, and not a rolled cigarette, be real? Or the Swede who was transported to 2046 while attempting to fix his kitchen sink? People were just too literal. She paused her internet search, more than ever convinced that that *something* was going on, and time travel fitted the bill.

Arthur's thoughts were running in similar vein. He had spent most of the day looking for his phone, without success, and after waiting on the line a mere ninety minutes and with only four transfers once he was answered, his provider reassured him that no one else was using it. He was still very reluctant to believe he'd left his phone in 1969, although now he thought about it he did have a faint recollection of a conversation with Edith where, in fact, he'd suggested he might be a time traveller.

'Gonna have to work harder,' thought Mish.

An idea suddenly flashed through Arthur's mind. Next time, if there was a next time, he'd try and bring something back instead of leaving something there.

'Bingo!' thought Mish.

III
The Atlantic Ocean, 12th October, 1492

"What was that fucking great bang?" exploded Columbus. "Can't you idiots see I'm trying to get some sleep!"

Columbus, captaining the Santa Maria, and his company of two other ships, Pinta and Nina, were five weeks into their first voyage across the Atlantic. At around two o'clock on the morning of 12th October the lookout on the Pinta, one Rodrigo de Triana, had spotted land and, as his duty demanded, had immediately notified the rest of the crew. The captain had verified the sighting, and in a state of some excitement had fired his ship's cannon to alert the Santa Maria. That was Columbus' 'fucking great bang'.

"Great news, sir!" enthused the first mate, Alphonso, unabashed by Columbus' vile temper. "We've spotted land. Or at least the Pinta has."

"What?" exclaimed Columbus. "Why wasn't I notified earlier?"

He scrambled into his clothes and rushed up on deck. Sure enough, a murky grey line bisected the sea and the sky in the far distance. Columbus had been vindicated. There was China!

"There's China!" he cried, triumphantly, to the first mate. "I was right! Those bastards back at home can eat dirt!"

The first mate peered into the gloom.

"How can you tell, sir?"

"Are you blind? Can't you see those pagodas?"

Alphonso strained his eyes into the distance. All he could see was a shadowy grey streak. But he knew his boss didn't like to be contradicted, and life was tough enough as it was.

"Yes, sir, I can just make one out." That would be something for his next confession.

"Of course," said Columbus. "I spotted it last night. I saw some lights. In the pagoda."

He had just remembered that his sponsors, Ferdinand and Isabella, had promised a lifetime pension to whoever first spotted land. He glanced uneasily at Alphonso, but his first mate had decided his prospects were best served by going along with whatever his boss said.

"Of course, sir. Last night, sir."

Anyway, Columbus thought in self-justification, a lifetime pension would be wasted on a mere sailor. They all died young of scurvy anyway.

Columbus had, in fact, hit the Bahamas, more specifically San Salvador (the natives called it Guanahani, but they didn't matter). The Bahamas was then populated by the Lucayan, a people with their origins in South America and a subset of the Taino, who were the indigenous population of the Caribbean as a whole. The Lucayans were described as handsome, graceful, generous and peaceful, and customarily going almost naked. The women were noted as exceptionally beautiful.

Just ripe for merciless exploitation by the Spanish, then.

Columbus, who was still convinced he was in Asia, although he conceded his pagoda might have been a palm tree with a luminous coconut on top, had named them Indians.

IV
The Caribbean, 12th October, 1492

A gaggle of Lucayans had gathered on the shore and watched in wonder as the three Spanish ships loomed into view. The boats anchored a couple of hundred yards out, and then a cutter full of heavily armed sailors dropped from each ship and rowed the final distance to land. The Lucayans, recovering from their shock at seeing these mighty galleons, started bustling around to organise a welcome party and send for their leader, who was called Keith.

By the time the Spaniards reached shore, the natives had managed to throw together a stew of their favourite vegetables, sweet potatoes, yams, beans and peanuts, with an array of papayas, pineapples and guava for dessert. The dishes were tastefully laid out on tables hurriedly brought from the local village. Keith, as headman, felt he should dress up for the occasion, and had donned his ceremonial palm leaf loincloth.

As the Spaniards landed, Keith, together with five similarly attired elders, and five of the village virgins, clad in their best cotton skirts, approached them.

"Welcome, strangers from a far-off land, thrice welcome," said Keith. "We have prepared a modest feast, as you must be weary after your journey."

The Spaniards, of course, didn't have the faintest idea what Keith was saying, but as a precaution, shot one of the elders. The Lucayans gawped in horror and incomprehension at the spread-eagled body of the old man; violence was unknown in their society. They had no time for further reaction as the Spaniards seized them, declared that they were now prisoners, and furthermore stated that unless they converted to Christianity within the next five minutes, they would be burnt at the stake. In turn, while the natives did not understand every detail of what was being said, they realised it was not good news.

That evening Keith was brought in chains to Columbus, who had established a camp on the island.

"Good evening," said Columbus, conversationally.

"Hello," was Keith's guarded reply.

Now Spanish is quite an easy language to pick up, and Iberians are adept at communicating with foreigners through very few words. This author himself has had little trouble in navigating Spain with a vocabulary of perhaps five or six words, including 'hola', 'gracias', 'cerveza' and 'huevos', interspersed with the occasional firmly rendered word in English. So, Keith had picked up a working knowledge of Spanish during his day in captivity.

"I have some good news and some bad news for you," announced Columbus. "Which would you like first?"

The Lucayans were eternal optimists, so Keith chose the good news first.

"Well, the good news is that your people have adapted very readily to Catholicism. That should stand them in particularly good stead in their future careers as slaves, knowing that God loves them and is looking after them."

The Lucayans loved a good fairy story.

"Now really, there's two lots of bad news. Unfortunately, your girls are not eligible to be nuns, because they're not virgins."

"They were this morning," interjected Keith.

"And the second bit of bad news is that we're going to have to execute you, because you were the ring leader of the rebellion."

And so it was that the inhabitants of San Salvador were lucky enough to be the first people in the New World, or Asia as Columbus still preferred to call it, to experience the benefits of Christian civilisation.

V
Croydon, May 2017

Both Jill and Arthur had reached an impasse on their separate deliberations about the possibility of his time travel, although at least Arthur had a plan of sorts in the event of a repeat of his previous experiences. But nothing very much happened, and life returned to norm. Arthur and Jill went about their weekday routines much as before; weekends were spent on occasional shopping trips, and the highlight of Arthur's month remained the meeting of the Croydon Beermat Society at the George, just off the High Street.

Jill had wondered whether to accost Arthur with her suspicions, but she knew that he was not very keen on the amount of time she spent exploring her conspiracy theories, and as week followed week without any further incident, the whole thing began to fade from her mind. Even so, one day when she was tidying up some of her drawers and she came across the list she'd started of Arthur's nocturnal utterances, she decided not to throw it away.

The only family member with an ongoing sense of foreboding was Mish. True, he had managed to alert both his servants to the fact that something was up, and his and his brother's comfortable life had not so far been affected by events, but he — very strongly — sensed the story was not yet done.

VI
The Caribbean, October 1498

Mish was quite right. The following day, one moment Arthur was sitting in the third carriage (his favourite) of the 8.18 to Charing Cross and riffling through his Metro, the next he was sitting in the middle of a Taino war council.

It was now the summer of 1498, and Columbus was on his third voyage to the New World. He was, by now, persuaded that he had not stumbled across some scattered outposts of the Orient, but instead an annoying barrier to that goal. It was five years since his second voyage, and in the interim Spain had been busily colonising the Caribbean. Not unnaturally, the indigenous inhabitants — the Taino, the Lucayan and the like, were a bit pissed off by all this. Liking a good fairy story, they didn't mind being converted to Catholicism, but being a fairly, free-thinking society they took exception to being burnt at the stake if they did not. Likewise, whilst their culture of being as helpful as possible to their fellow man made them especially good servants, they felt that traffic with the Spanish was rather one way.

They had attempted a couple of uprisings, but not being a particularly warlike people, had failed miserably against the hardened and experienced Spanish. But by 1498 they were getting desperate, and had convened — secretly — a war council of the chiefs of the principal islands of the Caribbean on Hispaniola. It was at this meeting that Arthur suddenly found himself in attendance.

The chiefs were not as fazed as might be expected by the sudden appearance in their midst of a white man in a dark blue Marks and Spencer suit (Jill had persuaded Arthur to change from dark grey to dark blue). Whilst the Taino had converted to Catholicism partly out of politeness to the Spanish and partly for the good stories, they retained their true belief in ancestor, or zemi, worship. Particularly notable and revered ancestors were responsible for key aspects of their lives, such as crop fertility and the weather, and sub gods took charge of individual crops. One of these zemis was charged with war. Now, being a very peaceable people, they had not really had to call on this zemi much before, but immediately before Arthur's entrance the chiefs were generally agreed that such a summons would be a jolly good thing. It must be said they were a bit taken aback both by their immediate success and Arthur's mode of dress, but then again you would not expect a god of war to look like a god of the sweet potato, would you? So Arthur, not having a clue where he was, was welcomed as a hero.

Arthur's total bewilderment was viewed by the kind and tolerant Tainos as the natural aftermath of Arthur's long and difficult journey from whatever region of the underworld the zemi of war inhabited, and so they adjourned for the day, well satisfied by their progress. Arthur was offered the most prestigious square hut on the island (square huts as opposed to round were viewed in much the same way we might view a detached house as opposed to a two up two down terrace), a feast of curried sweet potatoes, and the daughter of the local chief. He gratefully accepted the first two. He also received a briefing on the overall situation.

The next day, as the council reconvened, Arthur was able to make a surprisingly relevant contribution. His grammar school had had a Combined Cadet Force, and Arthur had signed up for it as the least bad way to spend a Wednesday afternoon. There were only about a dozen other members of this group, all united in their desire to skive off more demanding Wednesday afternoon activities. It cannot be said that morale or motivation was particularly high, especially as their battledress was at least twenty years out of date, and had been mistreated by generations of their predecessors, but Arthur had picked up the rudiments of modern, or at least mid-twentieth century, warfare, knew how to blow up a telegraph pole, and could strip a Bren gun with unexpected efficiency. Wasted in the civil service, this expertise suddenly found an outlet.

The Taino had another string to their bow. Individual possessions were rare in Taino society, and everything was shared. They had extended this philosophy to their current circumstances, and had relieved the Spanish of a substantial quantity of materiel. The Taino called it 'socialism'. The Spanish called it 'theft'. Amongst the stuff they had stolen from the Spanish were a number of primitive muskets, or arquebuses, together with the necessary powder and ball. Problem was, they had no idea how to use them. Arthur, with his proficiency in Bren guns and Mark 4 Lee Enfields, showed them.

VII
The Caribbean, October 1498

Columbus, through agents he had scattered around the various islands of the Caribbean, had been made aware of the spreading unrest amongst the native inhabitants. He was not too worried. There had been a couple of other incidents before, and the rebels had been dispersed by banging off a couple of cannons, and hanging the ringleaders 'pour encourager les autres'. This present discontent seemed particularly widespread, though, and so he determined to stamp on it once and for all. The epicentre of trouble seemed to be the island of Hispaniola, and so it was there that Columbus resolved to make his demonstration.

He began to assemble a force to land on the island, but immediately encountered problems. The Spanish settlers were no longer the hardened conquistadors of yore, but had succumbed to the easy life offered by the islands. His sailors were still exhausted and riddled with scurvy from the long voyage from Europe. Columbus could barely pull together fifty fit and willing men. Furthermore, their arsenals had been plundered by the Taino, and he could scarcely equip the fifty men he had. Nevertheless, he was confident that fifty Spaniards were more than a match for all the Taino put together, even if they were only armed with spud guns.

Arthur had been working hard with his willing conscripts. Mindful of Gideon's narrowing down his army to a highly effective elite, he had selected a hundred or so of the Taino who had shown a particular aptitude in World War Two battle tactics. This number included a handful of women. Those who had not made the grade as shock troops he had formed into a service corps, which was charged with relieving the Spanish of as much hardware as possible. Their efforts had even added a couple of cannon to the existing haul of several dozen arquebuses.

The Taino had their own inter island intelligence network, and had learned of the impending Spanish attack on Hispaniola. Arthur and his generals had the luxury of choosing their own ground, and luring the enemy to it by an ostentatious display of military preparation, without giving too much of an impression of actual capability. Arthur had not only drilled his men in twentieth century battlefield tactics, he had also learned from the Battle of Hastings. He had selected a bay surrounded by highish ground, where he established a strong defensive position. He would let the Spanish batter themselves to pieces on his equivalent of the English shield wall.

The Spanish task force duly landed in the bay of Arthur's choosing, but appeared in no hurry to join battle. Their first action on having established their beach-head was to set up a food tent and settle down to lunch, accompanied by several bottles of wine. They seemed to be enjoying themselves, and snatches of 'Y Viva Espana' and the Macarena wafted up from the beach. The Taino force, on the other hand, were getting twitchy. They wanted to get this over and done with and get back to their lunch too.

Arthur decided to force the issue, and fired one of his cannon at the invading party. The shot took out the food tent, which had the desired effect of deeply upsetting the Spanish, who had also been looking forward to a post prandial siesta. They gathered up their weapons, fired an ineffective cannon shot at Arthur's position, and proceeded grumbling and wheezing up the slope of the beach. It was a turkey shoot. A hundred yards from the Taino position they were caught in a lethal cross fire, and as they turned, they were bundled back to their boats by classic fire and movement drills. Of the original fifty about ten made it away in their boats; another ten, lay dead upon the field; and the remaining thirty or so were made prisoners, which in typical Taino fashion meant being invited back to the village to share another lunch and generally join in the celebrations of victory.

VIII
The Caribbean, Late 1498

As we have learnt, Columbus was not the most even tempered of men, but when the captain of the expedition (who had survived, like the Duke of Plaza Toro, by leading his regiment from behind and being first back to the boats when things went pear shaped) reported back on the debacle, Columbus went ballistic. Things were not improved by learning the thirty odd Spanish prisoners of war had settled quite happily into Taino village life, two actually marrying local girls. But Columbus was now in a dilemma. He had pretty well exhausted Spain's military capacity in the islands, and it would take months, if not years to get reinforcements from Europe. The Taino were obviously on a roll, and there were rumours that their newly conscripted god of war was actually an overweight balding middle-aged Englishman.

England was not particularly highly regarded by the principle European powers, Spain and France, at the beginning of the sixteenth century. The country had spent the majority of the fifteenth century in an orgy of self-abuse, otherwise known as the Wars of the Roses, and the fact that England had achieved stability and a degree of forward progression by the end of the century under the Tudor king, Henry VII, had not really registered in Europe. So the rumour that the Tainos' successful rebellion was being led by an Englishman was an additional barb for Columbus, as well as posing the uneasy question of what England was up to in the Caribbean.

The Taino, as might be expected, were cock a hoop. They were so pleased with the performance of their war zemi that they also made Arthur the god of sweet potatoes, as there was a vacancy, and in recognition of his English roots (the Taino didn't delve too deeply into the theology of that), named the site of the battle Les Anglais. Additionally, they presented him with an exquisitely carved miniature statuette of a zemi, with a war club in one hand and a sweet potato in the other. But they had no ambition to press their advantage and pursue the war; they were simply happy the Spanish were, for the time being, off their backs. And so the islands entered into a period of uneasy truce; Columbus and the Spanish (temporarily) too weak to renew the attack whist remaining bitterly resentful of their setback, and the Taino relieved that there weren't quite so many burnings and hangings as before.

IX
The Caribbean, late 1498

Columbus was still brooding as to how he might gain advantage over the Taino. He recognised the reinforcements necessary to crush the insurrection were months away, but how might he weaken them in the meantime?

And then he had inspiration. Sailors' health generally suffered in the aftermath of a long voyage, and a wave of mild influenza had swept the crews of his ships. There had been no fatalities, but there was no doubt his sailors were suffering. What if the bug were introduced to the Taino? He could then no doubt take some advantage of their weakened state.

He was aided in his scheme by the natural hospitality of the Taino, who were happy to let bygones be bygones and welcomed the sick sailors into their villages for their convalescence. Both sides, of course, were unaware of the devastating impact of introducing viruses to populations with no previous exposure. Within weeks the Taino were dying like flies from the flu. Arthur watched in horror as his friends died around him, he having brought a degree of immunity for himself from the twenty-first century. Columbus was delighted at the success of his plans, and easily reimposed Spanish control, although in fairness he had not meant to kill quite so many people. Quite apart from anything else, it gave everyone a servant problem.

The issue was immensely compounded, for Tainos and

Europeans alike, by two unfortunate coincidences. Influenza is a capricious disease. Most infectious diseases target the weakest members of the herd — the weak, the very young and the old. For much of the time flu did as well, but not necessarily always so. Upon occasion it would attack the young and otherwise healthy, and such was the case now. The youth of Taino society was very badly hit, the older not quite so.

The other compounding effect was a disease endemic to the Taino themselves. This disease was syphilis. Now the Taino, and their Caribbean, and indeed South American cousins, had been exposed to syphilis for hundreds of generations, and in them it caused little more than an irritation, albeit sufficient to make them want to distance themselves from anyone who had it. Quite naturally, the infected group tended to be the older members of the population who had been round the block a few times.

So it was that the recuperating Spanish sailors, who regarded sexual gratification as an important component of their recovery programme, really only had those older members of the populace to choose from. And syphilis was as devastating to Europeans as the flu had been to the native Americans, although being more of a chronic condition the sailors had ample time to get it back to Spain and enthusiastically spread it around before succumbing to its worst effects.

Was all this Arthur's fault? The Taino rebellion would have been doomed to failure had it not been for Arthur's intercession. Had the uprising failed, Columbus would have had no need to infect the Taino with flu, and while a good degree of coupling went on between the Spanish and the Taino under ordinary circumstances, that congress would have been spirochete free, the sailors being attracted to the younger members of the villages. 'Ah yes', you say, 'but the exchange of disease was inevitable, if not then at some later date'. Certainly, the natives didn't stand a chance. The Europeans not only introduced flu, but smallpox, measles and other viruses that were just as devastating. In the twenty years following Columbus' first landing in 1492, nearly ninety-five percent of the indigenous populations were wiped out by disease. But the rapidly diminishing populations, this time starting with the older members and given the particular means of transmission of syphilis, may not have infected the Europeans in turn. Who knows? Looking on the bright side, we got potatoes and chocolate out of the deal.

As things went from bad to worse Arthur's own defensive mechanisms kicked in, and he found himself back on the 8.18 to Charing Cross at precisely the same moment he had left. He blinked and looked around. His habitual companion, a man to whom he had never spoken or even acknowledged, was sat opposite him, engrossed in his Daily Telegraph and subconsciously grunting with disapproval at the latest machinations of the left. Next to him was the woman who had grown on Arthur over the years, despite her moustache. Nothing could be more normal. Until. He became aware of an uncomfortable lump in his trouser pocket. He leaned to one side, and after a discreet struggle tugged it out. It was a tiny figure of a man holding what looked like a stick and a potato.

Captain Bq'234@#zP

I
Space, 1962

The first mate of Andromeda Transduction Beam ZX80 carefully rechecked his instruments, and then, satisfied, messaged his captain.

"Earth in sight, Cap'n. One light day to go."

Captain Bq'234@#zP heaved a sigh of relief. He was glad the journey was nearly over. These long transductions played havoc with his digestion — not that he had digestion as we know it. His thoughts could now turn to the rather more constructive task of the job in hand, rather than mithering about whether he would make it to the data dump in time.

Bq'234@#zP, or B&Q as he was popularly known, was the recently appointed Andromedan Governor of Earth, one of the most prestigious postings in the Andromedan Sphere of Galactic Influence. The Andromedans had colonised Earth about sixty-five million years ago, shortly after the K-Pg extinction, and very much regarded it as the jewel in their crown, nurturing it from a devastated wasteland to the vibrant and verdant sphere it represented in Andromedan Year (AY) 100,000.057, or Earth Year (EY) 1962. But around two hundred years ago the evolution of Earth had begun to give the Andromedans cause for concern, and the root cause of that concern was man. Man had developed from an amusing little ape to an entity that built amazingly complex cities, sailed the oceans, composed heavenly orchestrals, wrote eternal literature and slaughtered his fellow man with careless abandon at the drop of a hat. But up until AY 99,999,857, or the eighteenth century as man amusingly called it, all that had taken place within man's own little bubble. It had not really impacted on Earth itself.

All that had begun to change with the advent of industrialisation, and two hundred years on, the pollution caused by man was beginning to look potentially catastrophic. Not only that, industrialisation had given man the ability to inflict such carnage on his fellow man that he was in danger of wiping himself out entirely. That did not unduly trouble the Andromedans; they would be sad to see man go, but he had had a good run and had provided much amusement along the way. What was bothering the Andromedans was that by the middle of their twentieth century humans had developed weapons of such destructive power that they could not only completely destroy themselves, but most of Earth along with them, and in EY 1962 it looked like that was going to happen. It was B&Q's job to avert this cataclysm, and his appointment was in part because his predecessor, Vice Consul PeR**$£BSc, was perceived to have been asleep at the wheel.

Man, of course, was blissfully unaware that Earth was an Andromedan colony, in much the same way that an ant is unaware that his fate is in large part determined by humankind. Man was not entirely to blame for this ignorance; Andromedans had evolved away from bodies several hundreds of millions of years ago, regarding them as unreliable nuisances prone to malfunction and ultimate failure, and now existed simply as a stream of consciousness.

Man had not been God's first attempt to create life. About half a billion years before he had had a go at man, he had created the Andromedans. But he had not been happy with his efforts. First of all, he had had no help from anyone else; the Holy Ghost had been as useless as ever, and as for Jesus — well! Secondly, despite God's attempt to create them in his own image, the prototype Andromedan had looked nothing like God's self-image, in other words Michelangelo's David. The Andromedan looked more like an influenza virus. So God had abandoned the project and had left the Andromedans to look after themselves, which was rather a stroke of luck for them, really. No mumbo jumbo about religion, immaculate conceptions, miracles and all that guff. Over the intervening half billion years or so the Andromedans had evolved into what they are today, which is so far beyond our understanding it makes God and his various mysteries look like a piece of cake.

"Slow the drive," B&Q rang down to the transport's Chief Engineer. It would take most of the day they had at their disposal to slow the beam down to entry velocity. He felt a slight shudder which signalled his order had been actioned; he was now free to finalise his plan to save the Earth. Which didn't necessarily include man.

II
Croydon, May 2017

Arthur had been deeply shaken by the find in his pocket. On arrival at work, he had surreptitiously checked the internet and had established the little figurine was a zemi typical of sixteenth century indigenous Caribbean culture. He could not put it out of his mind, and it didn't help he had a nightmare of a day at work. The government, desperate for overseas markets in the aftermath of telling the EU to naff off as a result of the Brexit vote, had done a deal with China to supply them with clotted cream. The big selling point so far as the Chinese were concerned was the alleged aphrodisiac properties of the crusty bits in the cream. This had long been an untested claim on the part of the West Country producers, and when the cream was granted protected status by the EU, the claim had been taken with a huge pinch of salt. But the Chinese were being very literal about the whole thing, and had insisted that the stimulatory properties be quantified. Arthur had organised trials with rabbits to see if the group fed with clotted cream had displayed randier properties than the control group fed on grass. No significant difference had emerged on sexual behaviour, but a large proportion of the test group had died of heart disease. Arthur now had to spin this in such a way to save the Chinese deal.

He was not able to give his worries full attention till that evening at home. His criterion for the reality of his time travel had been coming back with something tangible, and here, now safely tucked away in his bedside cupboard, was hard proof in the shape of his little statuette. Should he tell Jill? He parked that one for the time being. He didn't want to feed her conspiracy theories any more than they were being sustained by the internet at the moment, or at least until he had evolved a strategy for dealing with it. There was something else at the back of his mind. He had now had four events, and had played an increasingly proactive role as each progressed. Was he actually shaping history? And if so, going forward, could he actually shape it to his will? The implications were too awesome to contemplate. Arthur had a restless night, in which dreams of drilling Anglo Saxon soldiers conflated with being locked in a space capsule with Christopher Columbus.

He was not the only one to be having disturbing dreams. Jill claimed rarely to have dreams, and she certainly wasn't owning up to the ones involving Idris Elba. But tonight, she revisited her youth, and things developed in a quite different manner from actual history. Up until the point of meeting Arthur the dream was quite accurate; an exciting first couple of years at university during which she met and became heavily involved with Arthur's predecessor, Chris. Life was a great deal of fun, with lots of clubbing and trips to the Greek islands and Paris. She did not break up with him, and when they graduated, they embarked on a life of adventure. They spent a year travelling the world, then joined a commune in Yorkshire. They started buying and renovating semi derelict houses, and in their early thirties, with two children now in tow, established an estate agency. This went from strength to strength; they expanded into the south, and by their late forties were living in a very large house in Wokingham. It took some minutes after waking for her to realise she had been dreaming. She sighed, and went to sort Mash out, who was yelling in his customary fury at being shut in the kitchen, and make a cup of tea.

She continued mulling over her dream on the way to work. Why *had* she chosen Arthur over Chris? It was true Arthur had rescued her from an irresponsible hedonistic lifestyle in the nick of time and replaced it with one of academic probity. But when she thought about it, she hadn't done too badly in the first two years of her degree, and most people knuckled down in their third year with the intimation that the lotus eating life of university would not last forever. Maybe it was her parents. Jill had been born in 1964, and her parents had been early adopters of the freedoms and fantasies of the sixties. Attempts to tune in, turn on and drop out had rarely been successful, however, and the turn of the seventies had seen her parents divorced, bankrupt and nursing an unaffordable drugs habit. Arthur was certainly an antidote to that kind of outcome in her life.

She had never told Arthur the real reason for the breakup with Chris. Had she been too hasty to end things? The Tube pulled into the station and with a jolt she realised she had missed her stop.

III
Dover Castle, Autumn 1962

The Andromedan Colonial Agency had prepared a welcoming party for B&Q's arrival at their global headquarters in Dover Castle, which he much appreciated. He was an immediate hit with the existing staff for his open and friendly manner, and the old buildings were soon abuzz with flashing and whirling streams of consciousness. The human visitors to the Castle, trudging around wondering if they could manage the stairs to the top of the keep without multiple heart attacks, were of course totally unaware of the historic occasion unfolding in their midst.

B&Q's predecessor, PeR**$£BSc, had been in post for about the last two thousand years. Cool and aloof, he had been regarded as a safe pair of hands for the majority of his tenure, but, whether through general burnout or an inability to move with the times, was seen to have rather lost the plot over the last couple of hundred years. The events of the twentieth century, when man had succeeded in taking out more than one hundred million of his fellows, and now the threat to Earth itself, had been the final nail in his career's coffin.

B&Q received a formal briefing on the situation from his Chief of Staff, D*oM!!iNa//trix (call me Dom), the following day.

"Cigarette?" asked Dom.

"I gave them up about two hundred million years ago," replied B&Q. Andromedans no longer died; they simply rebooted every hundred years or so. "But go on, if you're having one."

Virtual smoke swirled around the room.

"Ah, that's good," breathed B&Q. "But to business. What are the challenges and opportunities?"

Dom found it refreshing to hear straight talking business speak instead of the Greek and Latin aphorisms his previous boss was fond of.

"We are in a critical situation," he began. "Man has discovered nuclear fusion, and is desperate to try it out." In Andromedan terms, this was the equivalent of giving a child a box of matches to play with. "It really looks very serious."

The Andromedans were by turn fascinated, exasperated and infuriated by Earth in general and man in particular. This stemmed in part from their intensely rational and logical nature, which had enabled them to become the dominant intelligence in the universe. While they had taken over numerous other planets which had exhibited some form of life, nearly all their other possessions followed the laws of physics and were intensely predictable. Earth was not. The Andromedans would never have foreseen, in a million years, that one of the few mammalian survivors of the great extinction that had brought them to Earth in the first place, a pathetic little tree shrew, would one day develop into something that could make an H-bomb, and yet maintain the same sense of responsibility as that tree shrew.

The Andromedans, while generally having a policy of leaving their possessions to their own devices, had tried to communicate with life on Earth. Their initial preference had been the plants, who they viewed as far more sensible than their animal counterparts. They did get frustrated, though, by the length of time it took to get a response from a tree, especially if it had to consult its neighbours. Attempts to communicate with the animal kingdom, and man, had been hopeless though.

There were three aspects of man's behaviour the Andromedans could not get their heads around (speaking figuratively; they did not have heads). First was religion. Why on earth was man besotted with a deity that appeared determined to act in diametric opposition to his best interests? The second was sex. The Andromedans had survived for hundreds of millions of years without such an embarrassing and messy process; what was the attraction to man for God's sake? It took up so much unnecessary energy. Third was warfare. Enough said.

"The world has divided itself into two factions," continued Dom. "The communists, who are led by Russia, believe in universal love and equality, and wish to achieve this by imprisoning and murdering anyone who disagrees with them. The capitalists, whose chief proponent is the United States of America, believe in universal freedom, and work towards this goal by subverting and murdering anyone who disagrees with *them*. The two sides are terrified of each other, but nevertheless are doing their best to bring about a nuclear Armageddon. And it looks like it's going to happen over a little island called Cuba. We are days away from the crunch point."

"Hmmm," said B&Q. "Your thoughts?"

"We could uninstall man." Uninstalling was the ultimate Andromedan sanction. They had only ever used it once before, on a particularly recalcitrant inorganic life form, and while it had solved the immediate issue, it had had such a catastrophic long-term effect it had made them extremely wary of using it again.

"Hmmm," said B&Q again. "We're going on a trip."

IV
The World, Autumn 1962

While B&Q had a very real appreciation of the urgency of the problem, he found himself strangely attracted to the behaviour of these over developed and reckless apes. They may have been wildly irrational in their behaviour, but they also seemed to know how to enjoy themselves, a concept Dom informed him was called 'fun'. The Andromedans had no such word in their vocabulary. B&Q wanted to find out more about them at first hand, so he and Dom embarked on a rapid round the world trip, focusing on the two major problems, Russia and America, and in particular their leaderships. Their first port of call was the Kremlin, where they found the premier of Russia, confusingly also known as the USSR, or even the CCCP, in conference with his deputy.

Khrushchev sat with his head buried in his hands. "Fuck me, fuck me, fuck me, Leonid. How do we get out of this one for Christ's sake?" He was almost in tears.

Leonid Brezhnev very obviously had no sympathy for his boss. "You got us into this godawful mess. You can fucking well get us out of it. Why did you have to put missiles in Cuba in the first place? What's the latest?"

Khrushchev groaned loudly. "The Americans are threatening to bomb and invade Cuba, and nuke us if we resist. I wish I'd stayed on my farm."

"I expect most of the world does too," replied Brezhnev,

coldly. "You will have to withdraw."

"But I'll lose face. And you lot will put me up against a wall."

"You should be so lucky," retorted his deputy, grimly.

"Seen enough," B&Q would have mouthed to Dom if he'd had a mouth. "Let's go." They slipped silently away to their next port of call, the Oval Office in Washington, USA.

President Jack Kennedy was on the phone.

"What?" he shrieked. "No, he can't launch a fucking airstrike on Cuba!" His Chief of Staff, Curtis LeMay, did not think there was any problem that could not be resolved by saturation bombing. "Who's in the firing line when the Reds retaliate? Me! Not fucking Curtis LeMay, who's buried in a bunker so secret even I don't know where it is." He slammed the phone down. "Is he fucking mad?" he demanded of his vice president, Lyndon B. Johnson. LBJ shrugged sympathetically. The phone rang again.

"Thank Christ. It'll be Khrushchev. He's gonna back down. Please God." Kennedy grabbed the phone. "Nikita, what... Pardon? It's not... Oh, Jackie, it's you. Look, bit tied up at the moment... No, I'm not making excuses... Of *course* I loved that little blue dress... It's just... Yes, and the hat... Oh Christ, she's rung off."

Johnson smirked. "Girl trouble?"

"Lyndon, I'm not always... oh, never mind. What the fuck do we do? The Reds aren't backing down, so we can't either." He slumped in despair. "We're all gonna die."

"Not Curtis LeMay," muttered Johnson.

B&Q motioned to Dom. "Let's go have some fun."

So the pair did a lightning tour of what the world had to offer. They were especially enchanted by the cinema,

Disneyland, MacDonald's, the Changing of the Guard in London, and the monkeys that had their own swimming pools in India. B&Q returned to Dover an enlightened and cheerier being. He had been impressed by humanity's ability to enjoy itself, even if it was accompanied by a monumental death wish, and decided to do all he could to save it.

"I've got an idea," he said.

V
Dover Castle, Autumn 1962

B&Q's idea was quite simple — in principle. It was quite evident that neither the Russians nor the Americans, or anybody else, wanted a war that would pretty well obliterate everyone and everything on Earth. What was needed was a face-saving exercise. This was very perceptive of B&Q, as an Andromedan would never have got himself into such a situation in a million years. When faced with a touch of humility versus total annihilation, the Andromedan would give a rueful grin then go down the pub with his erstwhile adversary. But he also realised he would need a human intermediary to achieve this, as humans were obviously immune to pure logic.

The question was who. Now the Andromedans were aware that there was a very unusual member of the human race, one who possessed the ability to time travel. Whilst that in itself did not confer any particular ability so far as diplomacy went, they just might as well pick him as anyone else. The only snag was that at that precise moment in time he was a couple of days from being born, which B&Q felt, quite rightly, might detract from his *presence* in the delicate negotiations to come. But then he thought, well, if he can time travel, let's haul him in from the future. So he did.

Arthur found himself sitting in the warden's office in Dover Castle facing Charlton Heston dressed as Moses, and Sofia Loren. As one might, he looked blankly at them.

B&Q and Dom recognised that they could not communicate with human kind as they were, in other words nothing all that tangible and light years ahead in terms of intellect. They did, however, have the ability, after taking a deep breath, to assume other forms in order to facilitate conversation and make their interviewees feel at home. Whilst in the USA both B&Q and Dom had been mightily impressed by the movies, in B&Q's case the films starring Charlton Heston, particularly The Ten Commandments, Ben Hur and El Cid, and for Dom, anything starring Sofia Loren. So B&Q adopted the form of Charlton Heston and Dom Sofia Loren. In doing so they had achieved their first objective, but the second was work in progress as Arthur shrank back in terror in his chair.

B&Q moved to calm and reassure Arthur.

"Cup of tea, old chap?" It was obvious he had visited England too.

Arthur's pulse slowed. When he thought about it, being offered a cup of tea by Moses was no weirder than some of his other outings, and it didn't seem like he was in danger of immediate attack.

"Yes, please," he stuttered.

The tea calmed him further, and B&Q introduced himself and Dom, gave a very abbreviated account of who they were, and began to explain why Arthur was there. By the time B&Q had finished, Arthur felt he might have something to contribute. Because of the circumstances of his birth, he had taken a deep interest in the Cuban missile crisis, and had concluded that it perhaps had not been quite so touch and go as people imagined, partly because the Russians were totally unprepared for war and were desperate for a way out. He also knew what that let out clause was.

The Andromedans were quite impressed by Arthur's knowledge and enthusiasm, but this now had to be translated into a workable plan to bring the opposing leaders together and hammer out a compromise solution. Arthur had an idea here too. He had recently been on a team building exercise at work. It had been a competitive affair, with two teams composed of Ministry food technologists and administrators. The technologists had, in general, a scientific background, although Arthur was the exception here, and the administrators were to a man Oxbridge PPE graduates, and, as such, had no practical or life skills whatsoever. They were quite good at modelling societies where PPE graduates occupied the commanding heights of power, though, as is the case in reality, of course. The two activities that Arthur recalled with the greatest fondness were a kind of orienteering exercise in Mini Coopers modelled on The Italian Job, where the administrators were hampered by the fact that barely half of them could drive, and only two of them had ever come across a map before. Once they'd got the hang of the basics of map reading, though, they did jolly well, although one team did finish up four hundred miles away in the Highlands of Scotland. The other exercise was making cocktails, where the team making the most interesting mix won, as judged by a democratic vote to encourage objectivity. Arthur couldn't remember who had won, so it must have been good.

B&Q and Dom were again impressed by Arthur's creative thinking, and by the end of the day Russia and America's leaderships, spooked by the sudden appearance of Moses and a balding middle-aged Brit in their midst, had been pressganged into attending a twenty-four-hour team building exercise at Dover Castle.

VI
Dover Castle, Autumn 1962

Each leader had been allowed to bring his deputy with him, plus one other, as Jackie Kennedy would no longer let her husband out of her sight, especially on a trip to somewhere as romantic as Dover Castle in late October. Khrushchev had consulted with Brezhnev, and they had decided to bring Tamara Press. If there was to be some kind of competition, they felt she would be a major asset so long as no one mithered on about what sex she was. Each leader was also allowed a heavy for security, at Brezhnev's insistence. B&Q and Dom were also allowed one choice each, and B&Q went for Charlton Heston. Dom chose Sofia Loren, which meant that there were two Charlton Hestons, albeit one dressed as Moses, and two Sofia Lorens. Despite the very real potential for confusion Khrushchev was thrilled to have so many of his Hollywood icons on board. In the general spirit of the thing Arthur was offered the opportunity to bring a guest, but felt, probably quite rightly, he had enough on his plate as it was.

Arthur outlined the programme and objectives. There would be two team building exercises, one outside and one inside, and then the final exercise where they would build on the skills they had learnt to decide how to avert a major thermonuclear war. The first exercise, based on Arthur's own experience of team building training, would be a 'Hunt the Defector' exercise carried out in detuned Morris Minors. The teams would be given various clues in order to find four actors dispersed around the Kent countryside masquerading as members of the Establishment, and using appropriate information gathering techniques finally locate the defector, or 'The Fifth Man'. Khrushchev and Brezhnev looked askance at each other, and the Russian security man ostentatiously checked the bulge under his jacket. The second, indoor, exercise, would be 'Cocktail Carnage', where the teams would compete to produce the most lethal cocktail they could. The Russians brightened visibly at that one. In the spirit of collaboration, the teams would not be Russians and Americans and would be drawn out of a hat, but with the stipulation that each team had to contain one Russian, one American, and one Andromedan.

"Any questions?" asked Arthur, brightly.

"Are you off your fucking head?" growled Lyndon Johnson. "Morris Minors? My golf cart's bigger than one of those. And's got more power."

But it was Khrushchev who hushed him. He was looking forward to sharing a Morris with one, if not both, of the two Sofias, and then the 'Cocktail Carnage' challenge.

Brezhnev raised a practical point. "There are twelve of us. And how many Morrises?"

"Two," said Arthur.

Brezhnev cocked one of his massive eyebrows. Arthur extemporised. "That will be part of the challenge. Fitting in." B&Q silently applauded him.

After much jostling, moaning, arguing and huffing the two teams were ready. Khrushchev was with LBJ, the real Sofia, Moses, Jackie and the American heavy (Elmer), and JFK had Brezhnev, Tamara, the other Sofia, Charlton Heston and the Russian security man (Yuri). It must be said their Morris *was* a bit of a squeeze, but Dom was able to discreetly dematerialise which created some more room. Arthur, as adjudicator, was to follow in a Land Rover.

And so, the cars set off around the Kent countryside in search of the actors and ultimately The Fifth Man himself, and on the whole, it was a great success. Yuri had to be pulled up for shooting the first actor who was impersonating a minor Royal. This meant the other team missed vital information, and Yuri had to satisfy himself with merely torturing the next three. It turned out that Khrushchev had bladder problems, and had to hop behind at least half a dozen hedgerows. At one of his stops the car got stuck in some mud, and Tamara proved her worth here by bodily lifting the car, including its five occupants, out of the quagmire. Even so, the two teams found The Fifth Man almost simultaneously, and their only disappointment was that it was not the real thing but a cardboard cut-out of, unbelievably, Anthony Blunt.

The 'Cocktail Carnage' was even more successful, and resulted in significantly less loss of life. After a brief introduction given by Arthur on the principles behind a successful cocktail, Khrushchev's team came up with something they christened 'Rocket Fuel', which was one part gin, one part whisky, one part beetroot juice and three parts actual rocket fuel. Brezhnev made an enormous contribution to the JFK team effort by siphoning some coolant from one of the Morris Minors. They were stuck for a name and consulted Arthur. After a moment or two he had a stroke of inspiration, and 'Back in the USSR' was enthusiastically endorsed by the whole team. It was a close fought contest, but 'Rocket Fuel' was judged to be the winner because not only did it render the most people unconscious, in some cases it resulted in significant brain damage as well. But by that time, it didn't matter. They were all too happy. LBJ and Brezhnev were singing to each other, the two security men were probably getting a little too intimate on the sofa, and Jackie and Dom were sobbing to each other about what bastards men were.

Arthur called the group to order, and reminded them of the real business of the day, averting a major thermonuclear war. After a slight pause, Khrushchev lurched to his feet, staggered over to Kennedy, and planted a big, wet kiss full on his lips (JFK was a little startled at this; mindful that Jackie was keeping a very close eye on him and Sofia, he had not drunk quite as much as the others. But he took it in the spirit of the occasion). Khrushchev turned to face the room.

"Comrades," Khrushchev slurred. "I have today been reminded of the universality of mankind. Russian, American." He turned and leered at the two Sofias. "Italian." Brezhnev harrumphed and gestured at Arthur. "Oh, and English." Arthur felt slightly miffed. "I will remove my missiles from Cuba. Tonight."

The room heaved a collective sigh of relief. Kennedy stood.

"That is great news," he responded. "And in the spirit of international reconciliation, I shall withdraw American missiles from Turkey."

Brezhnev cocked an eyebrow at Khrushchev. They both knew the American missiles were obsolete and were to be withdrawn anyway. But Khrushchev had renewed his love affair with America and was past caring anyway.

"Whatever," he said.

And that is how the world avoided thermonuclear destruction in the autumn of 1962.

Jill

I

University of Newport Pagnell, October 1982

Jill dumped her case on the bed and gazed around her room in the new build university residence. She was enchanted. A narrow single bed with a pretty green patterned coverlet, matching curtains, a desk with a little bookshelf and a chair, *and* an easy chair in the corner greeted her. She turned round. A built-in wardrobe stood behind her, and next to it a simple washbasin. And it was hers, all hers. She sat on the bed with a sigh of satisfaction. She couldn't really remember when she'd last had a room of her own, certainly not since the breakup of her parents' marriage, and that was over ten years ago. Home since then had been a series of grotty flats and even bedsits as she'd been shunted between her impecunious and irresponsible parents, sometimes lucky to even have a sofa to call her own. But now she was sitting in her own room, looking forward to Freshers Week with a mixture of excitement and anxiety, and due to start her English degree the following week.

There was a knock on the door, and Jill opened it to a freckled face framed by a cascade of copper coloured hair.

"Hi," said the face. "I'm Rosie. I'm next door."

"C-come in," stuttered Jill. She was inviting someone in! Nobody had actually asked to come into her space before, they just barged in. They sat on the bed together.

"You're…?" asked Rosie.

"Oh! I'm Jill."

"Your room's nice. I like green," said Rosie.

"Aren't they all the same?" asked Jill.

"Mine's all yellow. Doesn't work so well. I can see me spending time in your room."

"That would be lovely," breathed Jill.

Jill and Rosie became immediate and firm friends. Rosie was from the home counties, was there to study biology, and was much more worldly wise than Jill. Jill became friends with most of the other thirteen girls on her floor, but Rosie was the anchor with whom she navigated the first few exciting, though potentially perilous, weeks of university. Freshers Week passed in a whirl of wine and cheese parties, fending off either lecherous second and third years who viewed the week much as grouse shooters view The Glorious Twelfth, or equally persistent minority interest societies who wanted to recruit them for either Jesus or Marx. She listened to unknown folk singers till the small hours of the morning, and explored the pubs of Newport Pagnell with Rosie. Jill really didn't have much experience of men and relied heavily on Rosie to sort the wheat from the chaff, and through her good offices actually met a handful of nice boys, which gave her a weird feeling that she might actually have a relationship with one or two of them one day. Come the Sunday night the day before her university career proper started, she had to insist to Rosie that she really had to be in bed by midnight, and actually made it by one o'clock. She mulled briefly over the week; she'd met lots of new people, had only been sick once, and had not been recruited into a cult. She fell into a deep sleep.

II
University, Autumn 1982

By the fourth week of term Jill had a boyfriend. She'd never really had a boyfriend before. She had been a late developer, and had watched awestruck as her school contemporaries bloomed into young women. Even when her hormones started doing their duty, she remained petite and boyish. By her mid to late teens, if asked, she would have described herself as 'mousy'. She was oblivious to the growing admiration of her friends and classmates, who considered there was nothing that didn't look good on her. Large groups of girls and boozy nights out were not for her; instead, she had two or three close friends who spent their evenings around each other's houses listening to the emerging New Romantic music and moaning about Margaret Thatcher. A couple of boys had crossed her horizon; her school organised the occasional Saturday night dance, the male interest being provided by the local grammar school. She had danced with them, dutifully snogged them, and had even had a bit of a session with one of them behind the bike shed. She was much more interested in the music really, though. But despite the assurances and compliments of her friends, by the time Jill arrived at Newport Pagnell, she wasn't really sure whether she was actually attractive to men, or even whether she fancied them.

Jill's problem was lack of confidence. Rosie's was the opposite; there was no bloke she considered unobtainable once she had set her mind to it, and soon she was probably the best-known fresher in her year. Rosie's confidence was not misplaced, but Jill was the prettier of the two. Jill benefitted from the wash created by Rosie, and so met Jamie, the best mate of Tom who been briefly picked up then dropped by her friend. Jamie was from Manchester and was almost as shy as Jill. The few weeks they spent together were fondly remembered, but the relationship didn't last. Rosie had settled on one of the university's rugby players, and had dragged an unwilling Jill and Jamie along to one of the rugby club's post-match Saturday evening sessions. Completely contrary to her expectations, Jill found herself swept into the raucous boozy celebrations (the club had recorded a rare victory) and thoroughly enjoyed herself. Jamie didn't. That really marked the beginning of the parting of their ways. While Jamie suited midterm Jill down to the ground, end of term Jill had evolved into a very different animal.

III
Greece, Summer 1983

The most memorable event of Jill's first year was undoubtedly the trip to the Greek islands. Strictly speaking, this was nothing to do with the university as it happened during the long summer break, but it only took place through the friends she made there. Her second term had seen a distancing from Rosie as she found her own feet. She was still an occasional attendee of the Saturday rugby games and accompanying booze up, but she had migrated towards a new social grouping formed from people on her course who shared her enthusiasm for music and, of course, literature. Rosie had been put out by her protégé developing a life of her own, and the pair, while remaining friends on the surface, had lost the intimacy they'd enjoyed in the first term.

Jill had found a new boyfriend within this group, and together with another couple, Tim and Jane, established a foursome that was to remain the core of her social life until her second year. Her new man was called Dylan, a dreamy Welshman with whom Jill began to feel she might be in love. Whether it was love or not, she had certainly never had such feelings for anyone or anything else, except her rabbit, Florrie.

Around the end of the second term the little group decided they'd like to go on holiday with each other in the summer, and the Greek islands were the unanimous choice. Exactly which Greek island was left open; they would decide when they'd hitchhiked to Greece. Minimal planning went into the expedition. Through the student union they were able to purchase boat train tickets that would take them to Verviers in Belgium, which was only a couple of miles from the border with Germany. They were also able to purchase return air tickets from Athens for a date one month after their departure. They had passports, they were young, they were all in love with one another, and they were off to the romantic Greek islands. What could possibly go wrong?

They envisaged that many of their nights would be spent sleeping under the stars when not youth hostelling, and Jill, Tim and Jane, who'd all had some experience of camping, made reasonable provision including sleeping bags and some warm and waterproof clothing. Dylan, whose main experience of the great outdoors was passing out under a hedge after too many pints of Brains, did not. When they all met up on Victoria Station to catch the boat train, Jill was taken aback to see that Dylan's luggage consisted of his guitar and a small satchel containing his passport, money and travel documentation. She managed to persuade him to buy at least a couple of pairs of underpants before boarding the train.

The first night of the holiday was dreadful. It started off well enough: they arrived in Verviers mid evening, and found a little family restaurant where they had an excellent and very reasonably priced steak and chips Enquiring of the owners about camping opportunities, they were directed to an area about a kilometre out of town. Following directions, they found the turning which led uphill through some very dark and gloomy woodland. Trudging up the narrow path, they heard a blood curdling scream emanate from the depths of the wood. With an alarmed look at each other, they did a rapid about turn and scurried back to the main road. They eventually found a verge overlooking the motorway, and it was here that Dylan's lack of foresight became apparent. It had turned quite cold and damp, and Jill was very considerably pissed off to have to turn her sleeping bag into a groundsheet and her warm clothing into a makeshift blanket so that Dylan did not die from exposure. Luckily, they were able to adapt his new underpants as balaclavas. His offer to play a song on his guitar to cheer them all up did not go down well either, as he was considered to be the main cause of their discomfiture.

Jill woke in the morning stiff, cold and thirsty. Dylan, having expropriated most of the makeshift bedding, was still sleeping like a baby. She got up, went for a pee behind a conveniently located bush, and returned to rummage in her rucksack. She found a thermos still half full of lukewarm coffee, and a damp ham and cheese sandwich. Dylan had by now awoken, and was stretching luxuriantly.

"Gosh," he said. "I had a really good night. Anything to eat?"

"We can...," Dylan grabbed the proffered sandwich and downed it in one. "... share this," she finished, lamely.

She was more parsimonious in apportioning the coffee. Nevertheless, as the sun rose and warmed them all up, she felt better, and they were on the road by nine o'clock. They were hitching separately from Tim and Jane, who they'd arranged to meet in Brindisi in one week's time for the ferry to Greece. A toss of the coin had decided who went first, and Jill and Dylan had won.

The first lift was slow in coming, drivers possibly deterred by Dylan's large guitar. So they resorted to the age old tactic of standing Dylan behind a bush, while Jill, clad fetchingly in shorts and t-shirt, stuck out her thumb. Within five minutes a car stopped, driven by a student heading for Cologne who did not seem at all put out by the sudden appearance of Dylan and his guitar.

They arrived in Brindisi exactly a week later. The week had been full of ups and downs, which is a standard feature of any hitchhiking odyssey. Stuck on a roundabout in Cologne for nearly two days, in desperation they had taken a train to Heidelberg, where their luck changed, and a series of lifts had got them to Rome within the next three days. They had spent a day exploring Rome, then, both fed up with hitching, had experienced a chaotic train journey to Brindisi. Having been charged considerably more than their budget allowed for the tickets and then nearly abducted by the guard, Jill vowed never to travel on an Italian train again. But she had been philosophical about the downs, and had relished the ups. The memory of the lift from the German interpreter who was on his way to Perugia, and the beauty of Perugia itself, stayed with her for a very long time. Dylan, on the other hand, had not been a good travelling companion, and had moaned incessantly. What she had seen as a mystic other worldliness at college morphed into a whinging neediness on the road, and by the end of the week she was having serious doubts about the potential longevity of their relationship.

The journey through Greece wasn't much better, despite the fact they were now tending to take the local buses as opposed to hitching. On the twenty-four-hour crossing from Brindisi to Patras the four of them (well, three really. Dylan acted as if he couldn't give a toss) had decided to make their way to Athens and from there catch a ferry to Crete. It was a leisurely ramble across Greece though; they took in Old

Corinth, Epidaurus and Mycenae with a two-day stopover in a town called Nauplion, before heading for Athens and thence to the docks at Piraeus. They were largely sleeping in the open, but luckily Dylan had been persuaded to buy some camping essentials in Brindisi, which meant everyone had a more restful night. Jill maintained the hope that once they were settled on Crete Dylan's mood might improve and he would actually start to enjoy the holiday.

It was another overnight crossing to Crete, and when they arrived one of their first ports of call was to a bank to change some money (which from Jill's perspective was starting to run worryingly low). Whilst there they asked the bank clerk where was good to go, and he recommended a village on the south coast called Choridio. That was as good a suggestion as any, so that afternoon, having had a swim on a nearby beach and discovering to their horror it was adjacent to the main town sewage outlet, found them boarding the bus for the south coast. It was not an easy journey, and even Jill, who worked on the assumption that even the most reckless taxi and bus drivers didn't actually want to die, found herself gripping her seat and muttering a prayer as the driver turned to engage in furious political debate with the man sitting directly behind him while the bus swung at high speed around mountain hairpin bends. Three hours later they stepped off the bus shaken and white faced, and looked around, only to be taken aback by the reality of Choridio. A small harbour, a smattering of white houses stretched along the seafront, a couple of tavernas and a general store greeted them. It was Tim who rallied them, and heading into the high ground to the east of the village they found the most wonderful camp site, a grove shaded by a massive olive tree. They dumped their rucksacks, made camp, then headed back into the town to explore.

Jill thoroughly enjoyed her week in the little village, and even Dylan brightened up. The daily routine emerged as an early morning dip and a bit of sunbathing, and then a trip to the general store to get supplies. In the middle of the day, they would retreat from the sun under the olive tree, and emerge late afternoon for another swim. The evening would be spent in one or other of the tavernas, both of whose proprietors seemed to feel a duty of care towards them. It was all incredibly cheap, and as a result, considerable quantities of the local red wine were consumed by all.

Whilst Jill's relationship with Dylan had improved, she knew it was over. Tim and Jane seemed to be having issues as well. She had never regarded Tim as anything other than a good friend, but one night, after a particularly heavy session with the red wine, Tim announced he was going for a midnight swim. Dylan said don't be so bloody silly, you're legless, which was probably the most sensible contribution he'd made all holiday, and Jane announced she was feeling sick, but Jill really fancied the idea. So she grabbed her bikini and a towel and followed Tim to the little cove below their site for a swim. It was a bright moonlit night, and upon their arrival Tim announced he was going in naked.

"Join me?" he said.

Now, they had come across topless and nude beaches on their travels, and Jill had taken her top off once or twice when she thought she was at a safe enough distance from Tim and Jane, but when together they had maintained a prim beach etiquette. On the other hand, skinny dipping was the sort of thing that free spirits like themselves should do at least once and so long as there was no one else around, so she took a deep breath, peeled off her t-shirt (she hadn't worn a bra all holiday), dropped her shorts and knickers, and ploughed directly into the sea. As she did, she was a little disconcerted to see that Tim had had a *reaction*.

Tim charged in after her, caught up, and ducked her under the water. She came up spluttering, and flicked a handful of water over his face. In retaliation, he grabbed hold of her, and lifted her bodily out of the water before throwing her on her back with a great splash. It was great fun, splashing around under the moonlight. And then it happened. Instead of larking around, they were passionately kissing each other, Jill's legs locked around Tim's waist. She had never experienced such a wonderful moment, and she had no regrets as they emerged hand in hand from the sea and stumbled back to their campsite. If the earth hadn't moved, the sea had certainly sloshed around a bit. She did have a nervous, couple of weeks waiting for her next period though.

The remainder of the holiday was strained, although Jill didn't think Dylan or Jane had any suspicions about what had happened down in the cove, and when they got back to England Jill made it clear to Dylan that the relationship was over. She also made no attempt to contact the others for the rest of the summer break. At the beginning of the next academic year, it transpired that Tim and Jane had broken up too, and as they were all in digs now without the ready contact of a hall of residence, the bond between the four of them came to a natural end.

IV
University, Autumn 1983

Jill met Chris in The Flightpath nightclub in Milton Keynes. She had found a charming little house for her second year in one of the villages about five miles from Newport Pagnell, and was sharing it with three other girls from the university. These three, and their boyfriends, became her new social circle. They were more outgoing than her previous group, who had tended towards the local pubs, and she was visiting the nightclubs of Milton Keynes, or MK as it was popularly known, on at least a weekly basis. It was on one such Friday night towards the middle of term that she was approached by a good-looking dark-haired boy with a hint of Asian heritage. Conversation was impossible but they danced together till the small hours of the morning when he gave her a lift back to her digs. They arranged to meet again that evening, and the following weekend spent Friday to Sunday evening in bed together in Chris' apartment in MK.

Jill was smitten. She realised that any previous feelings she'd had for anyone, even including Florrie, were as nothing compared to the tsunami of lust and emotion unleashed by Chris. Chris seemed equally taken by her. He was similarly in his second year — Jill couldn't believe she hadn't seen him before — and was studying business and economics. He was indeed of mixed heritage with a Malaysian Chinese mother and an English father. His father was some kind of trader and his parents were obviously well off, as they had provided Chris with his own one bedroomed apartment in MK and a brand-new Ford Fiesta. Whilst Jill was agog at this degree of affluence amongst one of her peers, having his own place away from the university had actually distanced Chris from undergraduate social life, and he was as glad to meet her as she was him.

As the end of term loomed, the prospect of a three-week separation over the Christmas holiday filled them both with gloom. Jill had decided not to go home; when she had returned from Greece, she discovered her mother had moved, and it was with some difficulty that she found her mother's new address. Her mother had simply forgotten that Jill didn't know where she was; in fact, she'd forgotten she was out of the country too, so there was no malice on her part, but Jill, having to accommodate to yet another well-worn sofa, had had enough. She was quite happy with the prospect of spending holidays in her new digs, that is, until she met Chris.

Whilst Jill and Chris had naturally talked about their backgrounds — Chris' childhood had alternated between Asia and Europe, and in his teens, he had been parked in an extremely expensive boarding school in Sussex — she had been a little more reserved. Chris was certainly aware that her parents had divorced, and that she had spent the majority of her time with her mother, but she hadn't really let on about the hand to mouth circumstances under which both her parents now lived. So, when Chris suggested as a possible solution to their Christmas woes, they spend time at each of their parents' homes during the course of the holiday, Jill blanched.

"My mum's just moved," she stuttered. "She hasn't really had time to sort herself out." She didn't mention it was only by good luck she'd actually found out her mother's new address.

"No probs," said Chris. "We'll go when she's settled in. My mum and dad would love to see you. I'm sure." Jill heaved a sigh of relief that the issue had been (temporarily) kicked into the long grass.

They arrived at Chris' house in a leafy Surrey village (worth two and a half million pounds in today's money for Daily Mail readers) two days before Christmas. At his mum's insistence, she was to stay until New Year's Day, and given the house had six bedrooms, this was no inconvenience to anyone at all. Not only were Chris' mum and dad there, his younger sister, Lucy, was home from boarding school, and his elder brother, Charles, an army lieutenant, was also there. Jill was a hit with all the family, largely because her upbringing had made her very adaptable to rapidly changing circumstance and personnel. Her impression of the family was a little more nuanced.

Chris' father cornered her on Boxing Day and demanded to know what she thought about Margaret Thatcher. To be honest Jill had given little thought to Margaret Thatcher recently, particularly since she'd met Chris. The university itself was quite apolitical, and she really had no idea what Chris' politics were, although now she thought about it he was probably right of centre. Her own politics, not unnaturally influenced by her parents who were OK with Marx's 'to each according to his needs', but not quite so enthusiastic about 'from each according to his abilities', were vaguely Labour supporting, but she wouldn't go to the barricades over it. Chris' father was obviously a fan of The Iron Lady, so she cautiously enthused about the fact that Thatcher was apparently a woman, which seemed to keep him happy. Chris' elder brother, Charles, was clearly a chip off the old block. He'd recently returned from a tour of Northern Ireland, and sounded off frequently and at volume about the IRA, bloody students and the communists in the Labour party, when not ogling Jill. She was reassured by Chris' upward eye rolls on such occasions. She was also a little disconcerted by his mother's habit of wafting around the house naked. It was his little sister, Lucy, a very pretty female version of Chris, that she got on best with. They shared a love of music and Lucy was avid to know what was playing in the nightclubs of Milton Keynes.

Jill and Chris returned to Newport Pagnell a week ahead of the beginning of term, and spent an idyllic week in Chris' apartment making up for lost time in his parents' house.

V
University, Summer 1984

The remainder of the academic year passed in a romantic blur. She became a fairly frequent visitor to his family home in Surrey and was welcomed as a long-lost daughter, but she was always careful to mug up on Margaret Thatcher before arriving. She even took Chris to meet her mum, having carried out a discreet reconnaissance a couple of weeks earlier to make sure her current home was not in too appalling a state. Her mum was charm itself to Chris, and she'd actually managed to make her flat look quite cosy. Chris was suitably impressed and told Jill in front of her mum that he could see where she got her looks from, which made her feel slightly queasy as her mum fluttered and squeaked in response. He hadn't seen her after her third bottle of Liebfraumilch.

They spent their term time clubbing and at Easter spent a glorious five days in Paris. Despite the hedonism of their existence, their work didn't suffer, and at the end of the second year Jill was tipped for a 2(i). Chris was generally regarded as brilliant, and was heading for a first. In fact, Jill was secretly a little puzzled by his academic achievements. With his background and his obvious academic ability, what was he doing in a place like Newport Pagnell? Why hadn't he gone for Oxbridge, or at least somewhere rather more prestigious?

There was a reason. Chris, to the fury of his father, had been expelled from his Sussex boarding school for dabbling in drugs. Nothing terribly serious in the overall scale of things; a friend had been caught with a couple of ecstasy tablets and had named Chris as the source, and when his locker was searched a small stash of weed was discovered. His school was more terrified for its reputation than any proportionate response as regards Chris, and so he was out. He had to do his A levels at the local college, and they had suffered as a result. He had been deeply mortified by the whole experience, and had not told Jill. On their summer holiday, though, a far more comfortable stay for Jill in the Greek islands, he resolved to tell her. She was not at all fazed by the confession, and felt able to get something off her own chest. When she was eight, she had stolen a Mars Bar from Woolworths, and being a very honest girl, was glad that was now all in the open.

Up until their holiday in the Greek islands Jill had been swept along by the thrill of it all, and had not thought too much about the future. In her more reflective moments, though, she recognised that she and Chris had very different backgrounds, and as a result had rather different world views. In fact, their one and only serious row had been over the Miners' Strike, when Chris had been a little too triumphalist about Margaret Thatcher's take no prisoners approach. They had slept separately in their own accommodations, and a very minor incident had for some reason stuck in Jill's mind. The following morning, full of contrition, she had caught an early bus to MK to make up with Chris, and the bus had broken down. She had had to sit there for an hour in an agony of worry about whether she'd terminally damaged her chances. But, of course, she hadn't, and the exchange of guilty confidences on holiday really cemented their relationship.

To cut a long story short, they lived happily ever after, or as happily as two strong and independent minded people can do. Jill moved in with Chris for their third year, and as with most final year students, most of their time and effort was spent on their degrees. Jill achieved her 2(i) and Chris got his first. Probably the biggest cause of discord between them was what to do after university. Jill loved English, and was set on becoming a teacher. As the geographical location was flexible, she was happy to follow Chris to wherever he ended up. But Chris, much to his father's dismay, and Jill's too, wanted none of the capitalist world, preferring to explore the real world instead. "Think of all the sacrifices Margaret Thatcher has made for you," protested his father. Jill, as a result of her upbringing, craved security, which was not a remote consideration of Chris'. She wondered uncomfortably if he had been influenced by her mother, with whom he had formed a surprising friendship. They reached a compromise though; Chris would take life seriously in five years' time, to which Jill reluctantly agreed, comforting herself she could survive for five years in the open on a starvation diet. In fact, the five years were great fun; they spent a couple of years exploring the world at street level (Jill frequently thanked God it was Chris and not Dylan she was with), and then joined a commune in Yorkshire (where, it must be said, Jill occasionally came close to living in the open on a starvation diet). Around the five-year mark, as an evolution really rather than marking the expiry of their carefree existence, they discovered a joint talent for renovating houses. Significant money started rolling in, which meant Chris was reinstated in his father's will, and in their early thirties they established an estate agency. This went from strength to strength, and they expanded into the South. Finding the home counties far more lucrative (prices were starting to recover strongly after Black Wednesday), they moved down there, and their success, together with Chris' father finally ascending to the great golf club in the sky and leaving a third of his estate to his son, meant they were able to buy a very nice house (three million pounds DM readers) in Wokingham. So, by her early fifties Jill had all the security she could handle, two lovely children who were just embarking on their own careers, a Range Rover, and a lifetime membership of the LibDems.

She couldn't imagine it could ever have been any other way.

The British are Coming!

I
Croydon, June 2017

The only thing that Arthur had brought back from his most recent triumph of solving the Cuban missile crisis was a monumental hangover, but that was enough to convince him that what was going on was real. He again toyed with the idea that instead of being an innocent victim of events, or at least his placements, he might be in a position to direct them. As he mulled over the whole business, Mish jumped on his lap and fixed him with an unnervingly knowing stare.

Trevor, of course, had no view one way or the other. His only previous experience of commanding a genome was that of the mushroom that looked like an elephant's foreskin, and mushrooms are not generally known for exercising free will. He had already been over-ridden by some of Arthur's hormonal responses such as sheer terror, so had no real objection to being directed by his conscious aspirations. How to actually do it was another thing altogether.

On the train into work the following day, Arthur found himself musing about Jill. Perhaps it was their up-and-coming anniversary. He had always been curious about Jill's past, or at least the part that predated him. He knew, of course, the bare bones: her upbringing in the Midlands, her parents' divorce and subsequent struggle to make ends meet, that she'd had a couple of boyfriends, one of whom, Chris, she'd been very closely involved with. But he had always felt there was something she hadn't told him. Arthur had a pretty good memory, but the circumstances surrounding his (second) meeting with her were shrouded in fog. The truth was Arthur had always found it surprising that someone as attractive as Jill had gone for someone like him, and he felt uneasy that there might be undercurrents of which he was unaware, or had simply forgotten. He could not shake off this introspection, and he spent his journey home thinking in much the same vein. Jill was already home when he arrived, and he gave her a big hug.

"What do you want?" she asked, suspiciously.

II
Croydon, June 2017

Arthur liked to grow beans, and he would arrange a dozen or so poles opposing each other in pairs and secured at the top by a further horizontal to form a ridge. Mish liked to sit under the resulting framework, and meditate. He felt it was a special, almost sacred, place where he could be alone with his thoughts, and best of all, where he was unlikely to be assaulted by his brother. He could sit there for hours, and once the beans had grown to form a shelter, in any kind of weather. Mish was quite a deep little cat, and frequently pondered the mysteries of existence, particularly the peculiarities of his two servants. He had long given up trying to understand why their fur, or at least the female's, changed on a daily basis, but was now concentrating on the worrying other worldliness of the male. Of course, he was quite used to them both disappearing in the morning and reappearing in the evening, but the male now seemed to be moving in different dimensions.

His reveries were interrupted by a call from the house.

"Mish! Mash! Dinner." He heard a rustle from the bushes opposite and a scurry of paws as Mash charged towards the house, and thought he'd better get a move on if there were to be any dinner left.

Mish didn't often leave the garden, only occasionally venturing through the fence to next door neighbour's on the left, where he could savour the enthralling range of smells from other cats lingering on the shrubs, sometimes adding a contribution of his own. But one night, having spent nearly an hour in his special place under the beans, he thought he might visit the garden on the other side. The moment he left his little temple, something felt different, and he squeezed through the fence with mounting excitement. The garden was very strange. There was a sort of mustiness to it, along with a whole orchestra of smells he had never encountered before. As he wandered around in a state of enchantment, he glanced towards the house. It was nearly dark, and a strange smoky yellow light shone from the windows, not the clean white light he was used to. As he raised his nose to savour this fresh experience, a piercing scream erupted from one of the downstairs rooms.

"Christ almighty!" exclaimed Joseph Warren. "That fucking hurt."

Paul Revere gazed at the pulverised tooth in his palm.

"You'll thank me for this one day, Joseph," he replied.

Paul Revere, silversmith, engraver and all-round American patriot, had fallen on hard times, and had had to resort to his hobby of dentistry to make ends meet. He didn't have too many repeat clients, but his friend, Joseph Warren, physician, political agitator and fellow Mason, was a regular. Once the flow of blood from Warren's mouth had been partially staunched, the two friends sat down over a brandy and launched into their favourite conversation, moaning about the British. They didn't notice a little Burmese cat jump up to the open window.

III
Boston, April 1775

General Thomas Gage, commander in chief of the British forces in North America, sat with his wife in the dining room of their smart Boston town house and drew slowly, and with much enjoyment, on his post prandial cigar. He sighed, and exhaled a cloud of fragrant blue smoke.

"Christ, that stinks."

Mrs. Gage, once the society beauty, Margaret Kemble, and now a perennial thorn in her husband's side, feigned a fit of coughing. Thomas took one last luxuriant drag on the cigar, and regretfully stubbed it out.

"Better, dear?"

"Why don't you bloody go outside when you want to abuse yourself, and not make the whole room stink?" she retorted, ungratefully. Mrs. Gage had some quite modern ideas, not only on the health hazards of smoking, but also on equality in marriage. Her interpretation of that equality was 24/7 nagging of Thomas. But he was a tolerant man — too tolerant for his own good according to some critics — and he held his wife in the highest esteem.

Another aspect of Mrs. Gage's eighteenth-century feminism was to take a diametrically opposite view, on principle, to any position or opinion of Thomas', which, given the growing rift between the British in North America and the colonists, meant she was wholeheartedly on the side of the rebels. Like many intelligent women of that era, she was really quite bored by the routines of everyday life, and that had propelled her, quite dangerously, into an active role in the opposition to British rule. Her husband was blissfully, and possibly naively, completely unaware of this, and as a result Margaret was able to feed the growing insurgency with many valuable snippets of military intelligence, garnered from Thomas' unguarded chitchat in the domestic arena.

In the spring of 1775 things were coming to a head. Upset by years of British insensitivity and arrogance, the colonists, spearheaded by patriot groups such as The Sons of Liberty, were stockpiling weapons and making preparations for outright war. General Gage had concentrated his forces in Boston, and in mid-April received an order from London to take action against the American rebels in the utmost secrecy. And secret it would have remained had not Thomas that very evening over dinner said to Margaret,

"Guess where I'm off to next week, dear?"

As soon as she was able, Margaret despatched a message to her main patriot contact, one Paul Revere. 'Thomas on the move next week', she wrote (thrillingly in invisible ink). 'Will confirm exact date'. She was so excited she had to have a whiff of smelling salts to calm herself down once the note had been despatched by means of a sympathetic maid.

IV
Boston, April 1775

Mish did not respond to his dinner call, and was still missing the following day. By evening both Arthur and Jill were really quite anxious. Even Mash seemed upset, though that was possibly because he had no one to beat up. He also missed 'The Bed Game', which was no fun without Mish. 'The Bed Game' was an entertainment for two cats and one human, whereby the objective for the cats was to jump and generally frolic on Arthur and Jill's bed while one of them was trying to make it. If they gave up in despair, the cats won, but if the bed could actually be made, the human won. Mash regarded it as the highlight of his day, apart from eating.

While Arthur knew of Mish's predilection for sitting under his beans and had looked there several times, he decided to have one last look as dusk was gathering. The cat was still not there, but as Arthur withdrew his head, he noticed the gap in the fence on the right-hand side of the garden. He knew Mish did not normally venture out of the garden, and if he did it was on the other side, and so it crossed Arthur's mind that perhaps the cat had gone through and got stuck somewhere. Arthur didn't really know his neighbours on that side; in truth he didn't really know anyone else in his street, but he decided to pop round and ask if he could look in their garden.

There was no answer to his knock on the door. He hesitated, then spotted the side gate to the rear was ajar. The gate creaked open as he gave it a tentative push, and he cautiously walked through into the back garden. It was getting quite dark by now, and as he walked down the path, he softly called Mish's name. After a moment he was rewarded with a subdued yowl. Delighted, he turned back to face the house. The building, which oddly looked distinctly Georgian, was illuminated by a soft yellow glow, and there, silhouetted against one of the downstairs windows, was Mish.

General Gage had had an uncomfortable meeting with his senior officers. He had briefed them on the orders from London to move against the colonists and the need to maintain utmost secrecy, but had been shocked by the response. They had all but accused his household of being the main source of leaks on the military intentions of the army. Gage would have ignored it if not for insinuations he had been picking up himself about some of his personal preferences. Like many married couples, he and his wife employed certain spritzers, or enhancements if you will, in the bedroom to keep their marriage alive (very successful ones, given Margaret had eleven children). It was the detail of some of these little add-ons that had persuaded him that Margaret was perhaps not being as discreet as she should be. He therefore resolved that for the duration of the current crisis at least he would be more guarded in what he told her.

Paul Revere had been quite taken by Mish. He had never seen another cat like him, and had been captivated by Mish's immediate friendliness and affection. From Mish's point of view, of course, he was just hungry. Revere had to be careful, though. Cats were still regarded as evil incarnate by certain sections of the population, particularly the Puritans, and after all, it had not been that long since they had been hanging witches up in Salem. An unusual looking cat would stand no chance.

Revere had other things on his mind, though. It had been over a week since he had received Margaret Gage's message about imminent British troop movements, but he had received no confirmation about exactly when. He didn't want to trigger the alarm prematurely because that would have revealed the rebels' hand to the British, but he equally wanted the countryside to be ready for the anticipated incursion. He was in an agony of indecision, and hyperalert to any sign from Margaret that the British were on the move. The reason he hadn't heard anything, of course, was that General Gage had finally stopped informing his wife of highly sensitive military intelligence, even after she had offered to try out a previously forbidden spritzer.

Arthur called out to Mish again, and approached the house. He was a bit puzzled that the house appeared to be lit by candlelight and occupied when there had been no answer at the front door, but he was so relieved to have found Mish he gave it no further thought as he rapped on the back door. He was taken aback though when a man apparently dressed in eighteenth century costume and a flowing wig answered.

"Excuse me," said Arthur, politely, "I think that's my cat in…"

"You're English?" interrupted Revere. "You're on the move?"

Arthur was taken aback by the question. Jill and he had actually discussed moving a couple of weeks back, but not very seriously, and how on earth did this chap know?

"Well, yes and…"

That was enough for Paul Revere. The British were

coming! He pushed past Arthur, leapt on the horse he had kept in full preparation for the last few nights, and disappeared into the New England night. By the following morning, the whole countryside had been alerted to the threat and was up in arms. Unfortunately for the British, that was precisely the day they had decided, in the greatest secrecy, to march to Lexington and Concord to seize the rebel armouries and arrest the ringleaders of the insurrection. They met a prepared insurgency, were humiliated in battle and bundled unceremoniously back to Boston. The American Revolution had begun!

V
Boston, April 1775

Revere had been so anxious to be off that he hadn't properly closed his door. Arthur gave it a tentative push, and as it swung open Mish jumped off the windowsill and trotted to greet him with an affectionate yowl. Arthur swept him up, and made his way back up the side of the house, through the front garden, and then round into his own garden.

Everyone was delighted to see Mish back, including Mash, who promptly conscripted him into wrecking the bed even though no one was attempting to make it. Mish himself was glad to be back on familiar territory, although he quite missed the boiled fish head he'd been fed by Paul Revere. Arthur withheld the detail of their joint adventure from Jill, though, saying only he'd found Mish in next door's shed. It had been very different from his previous time travelling episodes, involving as it did another member of the household, and he had no explanation for it (actually, neither does the author).

Arthur also felt a little uneasy about his role in this adventure. While he had swung a wrecking ball through history in his previous excursions, relieved only to be back home when they were over, he felt a sneaking culpability about this one. He looked up the American Revolution on Wikipedia, and with a sinking feeling realised quite how critical Paul Revere's ride had been to the success of the early days. If the colonists had been caught on the hop by the British, the revolution might have been nipped in the bud.

He wondered if he could make amends, although the enormity of altering history in such a way did not really cross his mind, at least at this stage. He sat in his favourite armchair and concentrated on eighteenth century America. Nothing happened. When he went to bed that night, he fantasised about an adventure involving Paul Revere, Thomas Jefferson, Benjamin Franklin, John Adams and General Gage. The net result was a very satisfying dream about Mrs. Frobisher from HR, but he woke up in his own bed (he made a mental note to think about the American Founding Fathers when he next wanted a night with Mrs. Frobisher). As a last resort, he thought he might try and retrace Mish's route into the eighteenth century. He burrowed into his beans ("What on earth are you doing?" asked Jill), then made his way to the gap in the fence. After a bit of a struggle, he was able to wriggle through, watched by an increasingly perplexed Jill. He emerged into a clump of bushes, and as he stood up, was surrounded by Redcoats.

Arthur found himself in the not entirely unfamiliar situation of being frogmarched by soldiers towards an uncertain fate. In this case that fate seemed to be a group of elaborately dressed British officers. His escort stamped to a noisy halt.

"Found this person lurking in the bushes, sah!" said the sergeant to the most senior looking of the elaborately dressed officers.

General Gage turned wearily from directing operations at the Battle of Bunker Hill to the newly arrived group, and looked Arthur up and down.

"Who the fuck are you?" asked the general.

"Smith, sir, Arthur Smith." From experience Arthur had learnt no further explanations were appropriate at this stage of the proceedings. They'd either hang him or ignore him. Gage chose the latter option, and turned back to the battle.

Things were not going well for the British. The Americans had occupied a strategically important hill overlooking Boston, and the British, having little regard for their opponents' military expertise, had simply attempted to march straight up the hill towards them. The number of dead Redcoats littering the field before them testified to the imprudence of this tactic. Two assaults had failed, and Gage was contemplating how to manage the third.

Arthur realised he had landed in the middle of the Battle of Bunker Hill. He had read up on the battle in the course of his Wikipedia researches, and felt he might have a contribution to make based on his tried and tested CCF training. He also felt such input could in some way remedy a situation he considered partly his fault.

"Excuse me, sir," he said, nervously, to Gage.

"Are you still here?"

Arthur felt that was a bit unfair given the mayhem surrounding them, but he pushed on.

"Have you thought of fire and movement, sir? One group of soldiers dodging up the hill while another group covers them, and vice versa?"

Gage gave him a withering look. "We're gentlemen. We don't dodge and hide. We march straight up to the enemy and look him in the eye!"

Arthur decided to play the class card. "They're not, sir." He gestured at the exhausted and despairing rank and file waiting on the order to advance again.

Gage looked at him thoughtfully. "Hmmm," he said.

"You're right. They're scum. What school did you go to?"

After a little more detail from Arthur, General Gage successfully employed Second World War battle tactics, and carried the hill on his third attempt. Most unfairly, the Americans regarded it as a major victory.

VI
Philadelphia, 1775

It was happy hour at the George III, the tavern nearest to the Philadelphia State House. Three men sat at a rough wooden table in a corner of the bar.

"Another one?" asked Thomas Jefferson.

"We've had three already," replied John Adams. "We're supposed to be writing this Declaration of Independence."

"Oh, come on," said Jefferson. "It'll lubricate our brains. And happy hour ends in five minutes." He turned to the third man. "Ben. You have the casting vote. Shall we or shan't we?"

"Eh?" said Benjamin Franklin. His mind had been on his recent kite flying experiment to demonstrate the existence of electricity, and the belt he had received from it. "Oh, all right, if you say so."

"Christ, am I the only one taking this seriously?" exclaimed Adams.

"Are you challenging democracy?" responded Jefferson. "Two against one."

"One against one and one absent," said Adams sarcastically. "Come on, Ben, this is more important than flying a bleeding kite."

"Ben feels suitably admonished," said Jefferson. "I'll get the beers."

When Jefferson returned with the drinks, Adams had got out a blank sheet of paper. "OK, where do we start?"

The men mulled it over for a moment or two.

"We need to start off with something stirring," suggested Jefferson.

"Not something snappy?" said Franklin. "How about Brits Piss Off Home."

"Whilst I respect the sentiment, this document is going to go down as a landmark in history," rejoined Adams. "It definitely needs to be something stirring. And dignified. And lots more words than that."

Jefferson had been jotting something down on the back of a beermat. "How about something like 'When in the Course of human events, it becomes necessary for one people to dissolve the political bands which have connected them with another', etc etc, etc," he said. "That's effectively 'Brits Piss Off Home' in legal language."

"Brill," said Adams. "Can I leave you to pad that out? Next para."

Franklin chipped in here. "I've got something. It starts 'We hold these truths to be self-evident, that all men are created equal, that they are endowed by their Creator with certain unalienable Rights, that among these are Life, Liberty and the pursuit of Happiness'. What do you think?"

Adams furrowed his brow. "Not so sure about the 'all men are created equal' bit. That might be open to misinterpretation."

"What, you mean some people might think you mean 'all men', like, literally?" queried Jefferson. "Like Blacks, and Indians, and, God forbid, even women?"

"Well, that's not what I *mean*," said Franklin, defensively. "I mean chaps like us."

"Let's not worry about that now," said Adams,

pragmatically. "This is only a back of the fag packet…"

"Or beermat," chortled Jefferson.

"…first draft," continued Adams, ignoring him. "We can straighten it out later. What we've got to do now is say what we've actually got against the Brits. Our grievances."

There was silence.

"Oh, come on. We can't just say bugger off without some reasons."

After a further pause, Franklin said, "Well, my sister's daughter said that her best friend's cousin had been put in the family way by a British corporal."

Adams snorted derisively.

"They don't look after their teeth?" ventured Jefferson.

"Would you pick up your musket and leave your farmstead for the militia because a British corporal with bad teeth might have impregnated an extremely distant relative's best friend?"

Jefferson and Franklin shifted uncomfortably.

"Looks like it's all down to me again," Adams moaned. "Well, I've got twenty-seven."

"Blimey," said Jefferson. "This calls for another beer."

The following evening found the three revolutionaries sitting at the same table in the George III, each with a foaming tankard of Sam Adams in front of them.

"Tonight's business, gentlemen," said John Adams. "Is reviewing and ratifying the twenty-seven grievances. And can we please start on the first pint, not the third like last night."

There was a mumble of assent from his two companions, Thomas Jefferson and Benjamin Franklin.

"But first," continued Adams, "Ben, have you reviewed the wording of your second paragraph, the bit that says 'all men are created equal'?"

Ben looked down at the table. He didn't really like being bossed around all the time by Adams. He'd sooner have been flying his kite.

"Well?" said Adams, sharply.

"It's complicated," replied Franklin. "We can't really say 'We hold these truths to be self-evident, that all men are created unequal'. That's no different from Tory Britain, is it? Your farmer and his musket's not going to be inspired by a declaration that says after all this is over, you're going to be back in the same old shitty subservient position you were in in the first place."

"Hmmm," said Adams. "Any thoughts, Thomas?"

Jefferson mulled over the conundrum for a moment. "We have put it quite a bit down the page. It's not as if we've headlined it. If we make the whole thing stodgy enough no one will ever get that far anyway, and if we have to read it out, we'll just say it quickly. Nobody takes these things seriously anyway. Take 'God Save the King'. Half of England would string George up from the nearest lamppost at the moment."

"OK," said Adams. "If anyone asks, we'll say it's aspirational. On to my grievances."

"Can we have another beer?" asked Jefferson, hopefully.

Three hours later Adams finally reached his twenty-seventh grievance, which woke the other two up.

"Say that last one, again," said Jefferson.

"He has excited domestic insurrections amongst us, and has endeavoured to bring on the inhabitants of our frontiers, the merciless Indian savages whose known rule of warfare, is an undistinguished destruction of all ages, sexes and conditions," he intoned.

"Isn't that a bit harsh," replied Jefferson. "Merciless Indian savages? We're trying to buy them off at the moment. It'll just upset them again to call them that. And think what happened the last time we upset them. We weren't too gentle afterwards, either."

"But they are," insisted Adams. "Savages."

"We may need them on our side," chipped in Franklin. "If all this really goes to the wall, we'll need all the help we can get. Including the Indians."

Adams shook his head wearily. "What we are doing is an exercise in practical Christianity. We need to get rid of the British because they are hindering, nay obstructing, the creation of God's kingdom on earth, where men, or at least chaps like us, can exercise our God given freedom to do precisely what we want. And God's kingdom definitely doesn't include Indians."

"So are all your twenty-seven grievances based on obstructions to the establishment of God's kingdom?" queried Jefferson.

"Absolutely."

"So, is God upset that the Brits are interfering with our trade with the rest of the world?"

"God is fully in favour of free trade. Except with China."

"And when you say they're impeding immigration — God's all for free movement?"

"Yup."

"Even Indians?"

Adams glared at Jefferson. "If you're going to be such a clever dick, you can go and write the whole bloody thing yourself!"

And with that, Adams gathered up his papers, thrust back

his chair, and stormed out.

"Thank God we can go home now," said Franklin.

None of them had noticed the balding middle-aged man in the white shirt sitting at the next table gazing admiringly at his beermat.

VII
Boston, Summer 1775

General Gage had taken quite a shine to Arthur, largely because of his military expertise. It came as something of a revelation to the general that in the middle of a battle his troops didn't necessarily have to stand erect and unflinching in a smart line while the enemy shot them down. They could lie down (the idea unfortunately didn't catch on with the army as a whole who regarded it as a bit left wing). He did draw the line at the suggestion a bright red coat was not the most sensible thing for them to be wearing, though. Gage was also impressed by Arthur's grasp of the geopolitical situation (thank you Wikipedia, thought Arthur) to the extent that he wanted him to mingle with the intelligentsia of the rebellion to evaluate the progress of their plans. When Arthur protested, he didn't have an American accent, the general pointed out that most Americans didn't have one either. Hence Arthur's evenings eavesdropping at the George III tavern, where the tedium of listening to the twenty-seven grievances was considerably lessened by the fascinating array of beermats in use.

But for all the improvements in military tactics and for all the intelligence about the twenty-seven grievances (General Gage dropped off at the twentieth), it was obvious the Brits were on a loser. Gage put it down to the failed raid on Lexington and Concord when he could have strangled the uprising at birth; he was convinced security was watertight and agonised over how the colonists had learned of his movements. Arthur, of course, said nothing but felt awful.

And then he found himself sitting in his armchair at home, Mish on his lap and Mash shouting because the door to the kitchen was closed. As he fondled Mish's ear, a thought struck him. He had no idea how Mish had travelled back to eighteenth century America (not that he much idea about how any of his travels had worked), but the beans and the gap in the fence on the right-hand side of the garden seemed to have something to do with it. Mish also appeared to be a key player. If he could recreate Mish's steps and subsequent incursion into the eighteenth century, he might be able to redeem his mistake.

He leapt to his feet with Mish under his arm and strode into the garden. Mish was a bit surprised because it was time for The One Show, Arthur's evening ritual because he fancied Alex Jones, and even more surprised when he was shoved under the beans, followed by Arthur. He turned and sniffed Arthur's nose enquiringly. Arthur turned him back and pointed at the gap in the fence.

"Good boy," said Arthur, encouragingly. "Over there. Through the fence."

Of course, the last thing a cat will do voluntarily is what you want it to do, and Mish was getting bored of this game anyway, so he exited the beans and headed over to the gap on the other side of the garden. Arthur, watched by a bewildered Jill, wriggled out from under the beans, and was able to grab Mish before he disappeared through his favourite hole. He marched over to the other side of the garden, pushed Mish through the intended gap, gave him ten minutes, and then squirmed through himself. He stood up cautiously. There was no one around. He looked towards the house, and there, sitting in an open window with the smoky yellow light behind him, was Mish. Arthur softly called Mish's name, and with a relieved yowl the cat jumped down and joined him, then fled back through the fence. One last look, and Arthur stooped and squeezed back into his own garden.

"What on earth were you doing earlier on?" asked Jill later, as they were having their dinner. "There's a trail of grass and leaves and muck coming back into the house. And Mish wants nothing to do with you."

As Arthur had little idea of what was going on himself, he shrugged helplessly. Jill rolled her eyes, then said:

"Oh, I want to catch the end of The One Show. There's something about the American referendum on keeping the Queen as Head of State."

Sliding Doors

I
Croydon, June 2017

Both Arthur and Jill were on Facebook. Jill had been an early adopter, was quite indiscriminate, and as a result had two hundred and sixty-seven friends, some of whom she even knew. Arthur was the opposite, and had only signed up because his children had decided that this was how they were going to communicate with their mother and father in future. He had thirteen friends, including the Croydon Beermat Society and the Jewel of Bengal.

When she was not checking up on the latest conspiracy theory, Jill spent quite a lot of time stalking people on Facebook. One day Jill's laptop was out of action, and so she commandeered Arthur's. Partly out of courtesy and partly because she knew Arthur disapproved of her love of conspiracy theories, she deleted her history after finishing with it, but she forgot to sign out of Facebook. Some days later Arthur received a mail notifying him that the Croydon Beermat Society had posted on Facebook. He duly opened up Facebook, and was confronted with Jill's page. Now, Jill had absolutely nothing to hide so far as Facebook was concerned, but the site does recommend people as friends whose connection with the individual concerned make Six Degrees of Separation look uncomfortably chummy, and there, staring at him as a prospective friend, was Jill's ex, Chris.

It gave Arthur quite a jolt, not that he had any suspicions so far as Jill was concerned, but just to be reminded of his feelings of insecurity, and, it must be said, jealousy. His recent excursions to eighteenth century America had rather driven his musings about Jill's past from his mind, but the sight of her previous boyfriend reawakened them, especially reading Chris' profile — globetrotter turned highly successful (and rich) estate agent. Over the next few days, he became almost obsessed with speculating about her relationship with Chris, particularly the reasons behind its termination, and whether he could actually go back and find out more. After all, he had engineered two return trips to America, even though he still didn't quite know how. Mish had definitely been a catalyst though.

He didn't like to think about America too much; when he did, he felt distinctly uneasy about what he might have done. The media was full of the up-and-coming American referendum on whether Queen Elizabeth II should remain Head of State — it looked as if it might be a close call.

After a couple of days thinking about little else other than Jill's past, he decided to distract himself by checking American history on Wikipedia. It was pretty bland. There had been some unrest in the late eighteenth century, but it had been successfully suppressed, and the States had remained a loyal part of the British empire, then Commonwealth, ever since, even now it was a superpower. Every so often, as with other Commonwealth countries, debate arose as to whether to keep the Queen, or the Union Jack, or English as the official language, but the status quo had been maintained so far. This time the nationalist charge in America was being led by one

Donald Trump, whose 'America First' slogan had caught the popular mood making the whole thing very much touch and go. Arthur closed down his computer. This was not how he'd been taught it.

II
University of Newport Pagnell, October 1981

Arthur dropped his case on the floor and slumped on the bed with a sigh of relief. It had been a long day. He had turned up at the University of Newport Pagnell's accommodation office to claim his room, only to find they had lost all record of him. After several hours hanging around, a kind hearted lady accommodation officer had found him a room on a floor of postgraduates. He was warned though that as an eighteen-year-old on a floor of twenty, thirty and even forty-year-olds, the imperative might be work rather than undergraduate high jinks.

Arthur was not remotely troubled by this. He was a serious boy, and had actually been quite worried that his first year at university might have been all apple pie beds, traffic cones on top of statues, debagging and other public school inspired jolly japes. While serious, he was not particularly academic, and had really only gone to university because he couldn't think of anything else to do.

He was relieved when Freshers Week was over. He had dutifully attended all the introductory lectures including the one on birth control. It was not a subject he'd had to previously consider, but he was now a convert to the virtues of the Dutch cap. Wine and cheese parties came and went, and he even went on a pub crawl in Newport Pagnell with some of the other lads on his course, but come the end of the week he had formed no friendships. Looking on the bright side, he hadn't offended anyone either.

He found himself enjoying his English course, requiring as it did a fair bit of solitary reading. He did his bit in tutorials and seminars, again neither overly impressing nor upsetting anyone either, and establishing no relationships with other course members beyond the tutorial room. He was oblivious to the second glances of some of the girls.

He did make one friend however, a post graduate on his floor called Roy. Roy was ten years older than Arthur and was doing a PhD in something to do with electromagnetic engineering — Arthur could never quite get the hang of exactly what. Cooking resources on the residential floors were extremely limited — a double electric ring and a mini oven and hob, which was frequently on fire, between fourteen — and so cooking partnerships were established to manage demand. Arthur paired up with Roy, and it must be said they ate quite well considering, certainly better than they would have done in the vile university refectory. But what cemented the relationship was beermats. Roy was an avid collector, and Arthur became hooked. Some of his happiest memories of his first year were touring the local pubs in Roy's battered Mini spotting beermats.

To Arthur's immense sadness and regret, Roy was no longer around for his second year. He remained in the same room in his hall of residence, and for the first term actually felt lonely for the first time in his life. Perhaps this is what made him susceptible to the advances of one of the girls on his course.

Cathy was a tall skinny girl with big brown eyes and dark shoulder length hair. She had noticed Arthur right from the off, but having received no encouragement, or indeed any acknowledgement of her existence, had put it down to experience and directed her energies elsewhere. She also lived on site, and she and the other girls on her floor enjoyed a steady influx of males, two or three of whom she had had brief and relatively virtuous relationships with. But as the Christmas of her second year approached, she had no one to call on as a partner for the various functions and entertainments on offer. The English department was holding a wine and cheese do, and perhaps influenced by Arthur's general air of disconsolation, she decided to have another crack at him.

Arthur had had no experience of girls whatsoever, and wouldn't have recognised a come on if it had hacked him on the shin. It wasn't that he was averse in any way to the idea of girls; indeed, in his current lonely state it had crossed his mind a girlfriend might be quite nice. It was just he had no idea of how to go about it. He didn't know how to talk to them or what might interest them, and he was prescient enough to realise it certainly wouldn't be beermats. Cathy, having learnt quite a lot about men from the almost constant stream passing through her floor, recognised this, and simply asked him straight out whether he fancied going to the wine and cheese do with her, and Arthur said yes.

They had a very nice evening together, and two days later went to see Chariots of Fire. The following weekend they went to the students' union Christmas disco, and by the end of the evening were definitely smooching. Over the holidays they exchanged Christmas cards, and Arthur, perhaps in a reaction to the conformity and boredom of home, actually quite missed Cathy. They were delighted to see each other again at the beginning of term, and within a very short space of time were recognised as an item. They alternated their days and nights between their respective rooms, and Arthur was happy to show off his newly acquired cooking skills.

There was no doubt the initial catalyst for the relationship had been Arthur's forlornness and Cathy's maternal instinct responding to it. But she did find Arthur quite good looking — in a certain light, albeit subdued, she thought there was a definite resemblance to Charles Ryder as played by Jeremy Irons in the recently televised Brideshead Revisited, and when in the course of girl talk with her friends on the same floor she suggested this likeness, they said um yes, they could see what she meant. But what really cemented their bond was Arthur's empathy. Arthur proved to be a very good listener, in part because a lot of the time he couldn't think of anything very much to say anyway, and also because he found it difficult to get a word in edgeways. Cathy could talk for England.

They remained together for the remainder of the academic year, and during the summer holidays shared a tiny apartment in Ibiza. Whilst during term time they had spent a lot of time in each other's rooms, there was always the opportunity for escape, and they found being crammed together for a fortnight didn't work out too well. They had toyed with the idea of living together in the final year, but their holiday experience knocked that on the head. So it was that upon their return to university, Cathy found a house share in a little village about five miles from the university, while Arthur remained in hall. That did introduce a little physical and emotional distancing to the relationship, but given their energies were now devoted to their final year work, they — just — remained a couple.

Arthur did not visit Cathy's new home till the third weekend of term, when she and her new housemates threw a housewarming party. She had stayed with him a couple of times a week in the interim though because it was convenient for the university. Arthur was not a great fan of parties, and it was in full swing when he eventually turned up. Cathy didn't seem to mind as she disentangled herself from a huge chunk of a rugby player, swayed slightly tipsily over to Arthur and gave him a big kiss.

"Let's get you a drink then come and meet my flatmates," she said.

Warm glass of Piesporter in hand, he was introduced to Pat, a bespectacled second year engineering student. Pleasantries were exchanged, and then he was pulled over to another girl.

"This is Annabel," said Cathy. "Annabel, this is Arthur."

"Cool," said Annabel. For some reason Arthur was tremendously impressed by her response.

"Where's…," continued Cathy. "Oh, there she is."

And Arthur was introduced to a petite girl with shoulder length blond hair and wearing a short powder blue dress.

"Arthur — Jill. Jill — Arthur."

"Hello," said Jill.

Arthur was smitten. He could make no sound at all. His mouth opened and closed soundlessly like a landed fish. Cathy looked at him and nudged him in the ribs.

"Say hello, Arthur," she said.

Still no sound came. Cathy rolled her eyes at Jill, who said, "Nice to meet you," and turned to go into the kitchen.

The party really marked the beginning of the end for Arthur and Cathy. The chunky rugby player turned out to be rather more than a one-night fancy, and by the middle of term they mutually decided to call it a day. They would still have a coffee together if they bumped into each other on site, but it must be said Arthur's ongoing interest was largely angled, as discreetly as possible, in getting news of Jill. At pretty well their last meeting, Cathy said:

"Oh, Jill's got a new boyfriend, Chris. Don't see anything of her any more."

Jill had no memory of Arthur whatsoever.

III
Croydon, June 2017

Arthur sat in his armchair with Mish on his lap, and mulled over his analysis of his time travel to date. So far, setting Mish's input to one side for the moment, he had had no control over where he was deposited in history, but his return had been prompted by either a bout of terror, or a job done. The only time he had influenced his outward journey, so to speak, was through Mish's agency. He looked down at Mish.

"Mish, take me back to 1982."

"Pardon?" said Jill.

Mish just snuggled more deeply into his lap. That worked well, thought Arthur.

His thoughts were interrupted by a barrage of bangs. Mish jumped off his lap in fright and fled upstairs.

"Christ! What was that?" exclaimed Arthur.

"Next door's birthday. They sent round a note saying they were having fireworks," said Jill. "Are you all right?" she added anxiously, seeing Arthur's chalk white face. But Arthur was gone.

Arthur felt his way along the dank and filthy corridor, occasionally stumbling over discarded debris on the floor. There was a smell of smoke, and the sound of voices in the far distance. Despite seeming a long way away, the voices sounded urgent and panicky. He rounded a corner, and came face to face with a man standing in front of a pile of barrels, and holding a length of something or another in his hands. The something or another was smoking. The man had a sword by his side, and a pistol tucked into his belt. He wore a broad brimmed hat from under which escaped a tumble of curly hair, and he sported a generous moustache and beard. They looked at each other in horror.

"Guy Fawkes!" exclaimed Arthur. "You're Guy Fawkes!"

"Discovered!" cried Fawkes. He dropped the length of fuse, for that was what he was holding, and fumbled for his pistol. Arthur stood transfixed in terror, as Fawkes drew the gun from his belt, pointed it at Arthur, and pulled the trigger.

"Phut!"

They both looked at the gun. The dank atmosphere of the undercroft beneath the House of Lords had dampened the powder in the pistol, and it had failed to fire. Arthur turned and fled. Fawkes, horrified by the failure of his pistol to fire because of the implications for the thirty-six barrels of gunpowder and their associated fuses he had painstakingly assembled to blow up Parliament, hesitated. If he chased Arthur, he wouldn't have time to replace his damp fuses. The hesitation was fatal. As Arthur careered down the corridor, he ran straight into the posse of armed soldiers whose voices he had heard earlier. Alerted to the existence of the gunpowder plot, the authorities, so far unsuccessfully, were searching for the conspirators.

"There! Fawkes. He's down there!" he shrieked.

The soldiers caught Guy Fawkes as he was about to light his fresh fuses. Parliament saved, they turned to thank the balding middle-aged man who'd led them to the scene. But he had gone.

IV
Croydon, June 2017

Arthur's white face was as a result of his rapid excursion to the early seventeenth century. Having just nearly been shot by Guy Fawkes, this should come as no surprise to anyone. His exit and return had been virtually instantaneous in real time, and all Jill was aware of was his sudden apparent affliction.

"Are you OK?" she asked again. "Do you want some tea?"

Arthur nodded, and by the time Jill had returned he had calmed down.

"Was it the fireworks?" asked Jill, and Arthur nodded affirmatively. He was not yet ready to share his experiences with his wife, especially as some ideas were beginning to coalesce in his mind. Perhaps extreme emotion could despatch as well as return him? And could the destination be related to the nature of the emotion? He had been jolted by fireworks, and there he was, plonked into the middle of the gunpowder plot. But was Mish a necessary catalyst?

He was inadvertently given the chance to test his hypothesis the following day. Sitting again in his armchair with Mish back on his lap, he was watching The One Show and his evening dose of Alex Jones. There was an item on Bill Gates, and his warning about global pandemics. Now Arthur was terrified of disease. As a child he'd watched the cult BBC series The Survivors about the aftermath of a pandemic which had wiped out ninety-nine percent of the world's population, from behind an armchair with his fingers threaded across his face in a paroxysm of fear. It had scarred him. And as he watched Gates' doom-laden predictions, his stomach turned over and he broke into a cold sweat.

He was in a laboratory. It was night time, but the room was illuminated by the full moon shining through a slightly open window. There was no one there. It was cluttered, and as Arthur turned to look around, his elbow caught a little glass dish and knocked it to the ground. He picked it up and, having no idea where it had come from, placed it on the nearby windowsill. If it had had a lid, it certainly didn't now. And then he was back in his armchair at home. It had worked! A combination of focus, fear and Mish had directed him to a relevant time and place, and back again. Exactly where and when was not his immediate concern. Result!

Alexander Fleming tut-tutted as he discovered the abandoned and open petri dish on the windowsill of his laboratory. He really would have to speak to his technicians about housekeeping. Then he looked more closely at the plate. From the label on the bottom, he could tell it was a staphylococcus culture, but the plate, no doubt from having been left open, had been contaminated by what looked like a penicillium mould. The blobs of mould seemed to have totally destroyed the staphylococcus around them. Fleming's heart lurched. Had he discovered the holy grail of antibiotics?

The rest is history.

V
University of Newport Pagnell, Summer 1984

Arthur sat at his computer with Mish on his lap. While Arthur was convinced Mish was critical to the success of his mission, it did make typing rather awkward, especially when Mish got bored and got up to sniff the screen. In doing so he trampled over the keyboard and inadvertently invited several total strangers to be Jill's friends. For Arthur was back on Jill's Facebook page, searching for Chris. He reasoned that in looking at Chris's picture he could wind himself up enough, with Mish's mediation, to return to his university days. He eventually found Chris, and actually didn't have to try all that hard to work himself into a tizz.

Arthur was sat in his room at the beginning of his final term. There has been a lot of theorising about what might happen should you travel back in time and meet yourself. It's actually quite simple. There can only be one of you in a given time and place, and the time traveller's persona takes over that of the previous version of themself. He therefore knows everything that's going to happen between the new now and the point at which he left. In Arthur's case, he knew he was going to meet Jill (again) towards the end of that term, and they would walk off into the sunset together. His mission was, refresh his memory around the circumstances of their meeting and reassure himself that Jill really preferred him to Chris.

Problem was, whilst Arthur was by now a pretty seasoned

time traveller, and he was back where he wanted to be, he wasn't omniscient. His only source of information about Jill and Chris was Cathy, and he hadn't really seen Cathy since half way through the Christmas term.

Cathy was actually still quite fond of Arthur, and would have been happy to continue meeting up with him for the occasional coffee and a bit of goss. So when he sought her out on campus and suggested a coffee, she was only too pleased to meet. Despite Arthur's ulterior motive, they both enjoyed their get together, and said yes, we must do this more often. And they actually did. In amongst all the minutiae of Cathy's life, including her newly found love of Milton Keynes' clubs, he learnt that Jill and Chris' relationship seemed to be the real deal, and they were planning on living together for their final year.

Cathy's affair with her chunky rugby player had run its course, and she was once again between men. She felt comfortable with Arthur, and the fact that he had had no real friendships since his breakup with Cathy found them drawing closer together. One evening in late May, just as Arthur was thinking about going to bed, there was a knock on his door, and he opened it to a tipsy Cathy. She'd been over the bar for one of her mate's birthdays, had missed the last bus out to her house, and could she sleep on Arthur's floor? Overnight, the inevitable happened.

Arthur woke up with Cathy beside him in the narrow bed with highly conflated feelings. This was definitely not in the plan. But he and Cathy were both free agents, he liked her and she liked him, and somehow or another events would conspire for him to meet and win Jill because that is what happened. And so they resumed their affair, albeit on a semidetached basis. Come the end of term, it was agreed they would both go their separate ways.

As the end of term approached, Arthur started to feel twinges of anxiety. He began to realise that the whole idea behind his return to his university life to explore Jill's feelings for Chris as opposed to himself was a non-starter, if only because the only person who knew that was Jill herself, and he did not know Jill. He still gleaned a certain amount of information from Cathy, but that was limited to an outsider's view of the relationship. She knew no more intimate details than he did.

Two weeks from the end of term he booked tickets for the barn dance at which he was to meet Jill. It was to be held on the last Saturday of term, and he planned to go home the following Wednesday. Cathy was unable to go, having a farewell dinner booked with her university girlfriends. As the date of the dance approached, he felt a mixture of excitement and apprehension. He knew that that was where he would meet Jill, because, as he kept telling himself, that is what happened. Had he not known that for a fact, he would have been in despair. There was absolutely no other indication it was on the cards.

The dance came and went, and it did not happen. Jill was simply not there. In fact, Arthur heard the day after from Cathy that Jill and Chris had already departed together for a holiday in the Greek islands. Arthur was dismayed. What had happened? What had gone wrong? And far more importantly, what did this mean for his future?

He was still in a state of shock when he and Cathy went out for a farewell meal the evening before he was to go home, only to receive another shock. Their parting, which had been on the cards all along, was perfectly amicable, but Cathy wanted to get something off her chest. In early June she had gone clubbing in Milton Keynes, and to her surprise had met Chris, alone. It seemed he had had a row with Jill, and was seeking consolation in the deafening music and some mind-altering substances. As the night progressed, he also sought consolation in Cathy. When they woke up together the following morning in his nearby apartment, they both felt terrible about what had happened. Cathy hurriedly dressed and left the flat, only by the most enormous stroke of luck avoiding Jill, who had obviously arrived to make up. It seemed she had been delayed by a broken-down bus, and Cathy shuddered to think what might have happened otherwise. Judging by the fact that Jill's behaviour towards Cathy was unchanged, it would appear she was unaware of the incident. Thanks, said Cathy, I had to tell someone.

Arthur returned home in a terrible state, and promptly retreated to his room. His parents, who'd been mildly interested to learn of how he'd got on at university, saw nothing unusual in this and so were not unduly put out. It had only gradually dawned on him the awful dilemma he was in. At first, he was distraught at what had happened, or rather not happened, at the dance and what it meant for his future. He then realised that that alternative future was at present a fact, and what would he return to? Finally, what would propel him, backwards or forwards, from his current time slot?

It was Margaret Thatcher that came to his rescue. Although not really a political animal, he was so enraged by her triumphalism over the Miners' Strike, and his parents' enthusiastic endorsement of it, that he suddenly found himself back in his room at university a month earlier. He hadn't even needed Mish.

The following day, the first Friday of the month, Cathy asked him if he fancied going clubbing with her that evening. She knew he was not a great fan, but he had been with her on a couple of occasions so he might. When he said no, he was tired, she asked if he minded her going anyway, and was a little taken aback by how enthusiastic he was that she should. For it had occurred to Arthur that this was probably the occasion she had met and offered her consolations to Chris, and that opportunity lay therein.

Despite the fact that he lived on campus and had no real need, at the beginning of the year he had bought himself a car. It was a fifteen-year-old Hillman Imp, an eccentric little car that took ages to start because the revolutionary automatic choke had seized up years ago, had a top speed of 45mph otherwise it overheated, and had to be in a good mood to stop because of frequent brake failure. Arthur loved it, though, and mainly used it to potter around the local pubs in pursuit of the perfect beermat. On the Saturday morning, though, he was up bright and early, and having allowed twenty minutes to start the Imp, was on the road by eight o'clock. He drove out to Cathy's village, and there, waiting at the bus stop, was Jill. He had struck lucky. It was the morning after the night before's infidelity. He pulled up alongside her and wound down the window.

"Hello," he said. "Are you going to MK? Can I give you a lift?"

Jill peered into the car.

"Hello, er…," she said, uncertainly.

"It's Arthur," said Arthur. "I'm Cathy's boyfriend. We met at the housewarming."

"Oh, OK. I mean thanks." And she hopped into the car.

Jill fled Chris' apartment in floods of tears, the image of a horrified Chris and Cathy sitting in bed together imprinted on her brain. Ignoring his desperately apologetic pleas, she decided to have nothing further to do with him. She had been let down all her life by her parents, and she was not going to re-enter that nightmare scenario with any partner, even Chris. She was not going to continue to share a house with Cathy either, and it was her old friend from her first year, Rosie, who came to her rescue. Rosie shared a house not far from Jill's, and she let Jill sleep on a sofa for the last few weeks of term (nothing new there, then, thought Jill). She offered a sympathetic shoulder for Jill to sob on while agreeing what utter and complete bastards men were, particularly the good-looking ones, and made a mental note to look Chris up after a decent interval had elapsed.

Most of June was occupied with end of year exams, which at least took her mind off her situation, but when she did think about it her overwhelming reaction was anger. So, when towards the end of term, exams out of the way, Rosie announced that she and her friends were going to a barn dance, it was bound to be a hoot, and would she like to come, Jill readily accepted. It was great fun. And in one do-si-do, she was partnered by the chap whom she recognised as having given her the lift into Milton Keynes on that fateful day a couple of weeks ago. The dance progressed to a swing, he was a little too enthusiastic, and they both fell over.

"You're Arthur," she said, giggling on the floor.

VII
Croydon, June 2017

Arthur sat in his armchair, Mish on his lap. Jill sat opposite him with her laptop. She wore a puzzled expression on her face.

"That's strange," she said. "I've got a lot of new Facebook friends."

Mish gave Arthur a hard look.

La Peste

I
Brighton Beach, June 2017

Arthur sat on the seafront at Brighton and gazed at the pier. He had decided he needed some time to himself, and so had taken the day off and caught the train to the seaside. He had not told Jill. He was beginning to feel very uncomfortable about the position he was in. His trips to the past, with the exception of the constitutional position of the United States, had not altered the world as he knew it. But it was dawning on him that the world, and his marriage, might be in a very different place had it not been for his interventions, accidental or otherwise. What might he be responsible for going forwards?

He had also started having dreams again — very vivid dreams, with almost impossible levels of detail in them. They must have been influenced by Bill Gates because they were about disease, a disease that had swept the world causing unimaginable death and dislocation, just like in The Survivors. Boris Johnson was involved, looking distinctly the worse for wear, criminal organisations were making more profit from toilet roll than heroin and the streets of major cities were deserted apart from roving gangs of goats. The disease was called Covid-19, which sounded like a cross between a seventies punk band and a foreign intelligence service. In his dreams he could read newspapers with dates on them — on

23rd March, 2020 the whole of the UK had gone under house arrest, for instance. Dreams were how the whole thing had started when he began going back in time. Was he starting to go forward as well?

He didn't know what to do, and he couldn't share it with Jill. What if she found out that, but for his interference, she would still be with Chris, or at least not with him? It didn't bear thinking about. He got up from his bench and went to console himself with some fish and chips.

Arthur was not the only one worried about his impact on history. Captain B&Q had been keeping an increasingly watchful eye on behalf of The Andromedan Colonial Agency. B&Q had been grateful for Arthur's role in preventing the world blowing itself up in 1962, but even then, had had twinges of doubt about, let's face it, a semi domesticated ape having the powers that Arthur had. Since then, he had watched with increasing concern as the tides of history had been reversed or, at the very least, heavily tampered with. And now it seemed the future was under threat as well as the past. B&Q sank back in his chair (in as much as an entity without form or substance can sink back in a chair) in Dover Castle and thought thoughtful thoughts.

"Hello dear," said Jill to Arthur when he got home. "Can't be fagged to cook, so I thought we'd get something from the chippy. Your usual?"

Arthur slipped most of it to Mash, who couldn't believe his luck.

II
Ministry of Peace, Beijing, January 2020

The Minister of Peace, Chen Fung Fong, started at the abrupt rap on his office door, and rapidly exited his game of Candy Crush Soda Saga. The door was flung open, and his aide announced the arrival of the representative from the Ministry of Science.

"Come in, come in," said Chen. "Mr…?"

"Chou Li Mein," replied the youthful scientist.

"Sit down, sit down."

Chou confidently assumed his seat.

"Tea? The new season's leaf is in," offered Chen.

"Skinny latte, if I may," replied Chou.

Chen looked blank, but his aide scurried into the antechamber where the refreshments were kept. Must ask him how to work that new coffee machine, thought Chen. Not that Chen drank anything apart from green tea, but it might impress the powers that be if he could whiz them up something from the thing. Show them how modern and progressive he was, not some superannuated communist fossil from the last century. Chen had been having intimations of mortality.

"Minister?" Chen wrenched himself back from thoughts of the coffee machine and tried to remember why the young man sitting in front of him was there. It must be something to do with his brief as Minister of Peace, which, he reminded himself, was the promotion and preservation of world harmony. The Ministry was, in fact, a dumping ground for all the stuff that no-one else could be bothered with, but out of courtesy he was intermittently updated with affairs of considerably more importance to the state. The young man was a scientist, so it must be connected with science. So many balls to keep in the air! The aide returned with the coffee, and plonked a paper in front of Chen.

"The agenda, sir."

Chen smiled at him gratefully. He'll go far, he thought. Chen studied the agenda.

"First up, 5G," he read. "How is overseas penetration — er, sales — going?"

"Beyond expectation, Minister," replied Chou. "Prime Minister Johnson of the UK has announced it is to extend Huawei 5G further into its communication networks. Even though President Trump is telling him not to, and is threatening to withdraw his offer of sending his hair stylist to London.

"Er, Johnson?" wavered Chen.

"The new British prime minister, Boris Johnson. Elected by a landslide in December."

"Good job we don't have to bother about that sort of thing," chuckled Chen. "Excellent. Agenda point 2. Update on research in the Wuhan Institute of Microbiology."

"We have screened a variety of agents from animals that might escape into the general population through our urban wet markets, and we have identified no threats so far. Next up are bats."

"Bats?" asked Chen. "Does anyone still eat bats?"

"Absolute delicacy down there. Sweet and sour bat, crispy fried bat, black bean bat. The list is endless."

"Ew," said Chen, who was tinkering with the idea of

vegetarianism. He'd been very impressed by Greta Thunberg. "I assume security is rock solid?"

"Indeed," said Chou.

But Chou knew he was losing the Minister. He had slumped in his chair and his eyelids were drooping. If only he'd learn to work that bloody drinks' machine, he thought, he could keep himself awake with coffee.

III
Croydon, Saturday, 10th June, 2017

Mish had enjoyed his trip back to eighteenth century Boston, although of course he didn't know that that was what he had done. What he did know was that he had been spiritually refreshed by spending quality time under Arthur's beans, had had the excitement of going through the right-hand fence instead of the left, had entered a garden then a house saturated with enchanting new smells, and finally had met a nice man who had fed him fish heads. He told Mash all about it, and Mash was particularly taken with the story of the fish heads. He made Mish repeat it several times on pain of a beating up if he didn't.

One Saturday morning Mish decided to see if he could repeat the experience. He sat under the beans for a while, then wriggled through the fence on the right-hand side of the garden. To his disappointment the interesting smells had gone, and there was no nice man offering fish heads. He returned to his own garden, and went back inside the house to find Arthur, who was sat in his armchair reading the paper. Mish jumped onto Arthur's lap and then his shoulder, and stuck his snout into Arthur's ear to announce his arrival.

Arthur was startled to have Mish's wet nose thrust firmly into his ear. He was reading about the aftermath of the general election held two days earlier, when Theresa May and the Conservatives had unexpectedly lost their Commons majority, pushing the whole Brexit process firmly back up in the air. What a mess, thought Arthur. He was by no means a political animal, but he had voted Leave in the 2016 referendum. On reflection, he didn't really know why. He wasn't particularly interested in the EU, but the government had insisted he express an opinion, and he had taken exception to David Cameron and George Osborne's doom mongering if he didn't toe the line. Mind you, he didn't much like the Leavers either, particularly that Farage. Jill, on the other hand, had voted Remain, because she disliked the Leave leaders like Boris Johnson even more than she did David Cameron. There was no discord between them over their marginally differing views.

But Arthur did not like a mess, and that, together with Mish's aural attentions, could explain what happened next. Instead of reading speculation about whether Theresa May was going to resign or not, the headline was screaming about hundreds of thousands of deaths in the UK and worldwide from something called coronavirus. A haggard Boris Johnson stared out from the front page, and an opinion poll said that half of the population of England were too terrified to leave their homes even when lockdown finished (what's lockdown? thought Arthur). He looked at the date on the paper, and a chill ran down his spine. It was Saturday, 25th April, 2020.

He realised he had jumped forward nearly three years. But he was still sat in his armchair and in his own living room, although Mish was no longer on his lap, and there was no sign of Mash either.

"Jill?" he called, cautiously.

There was no response. He levered himself up from his chair, and went into the kitchen. A misshapen loaf sat on the kitchen table together with a printed note. Don't people write any more? thought Arthur. 'Have popped out to Co-op', it read. 'WhatsApp group reports they have eggs *and* tinned tomatoes. Back soon. PS What do you think of my loaf? PPS don't forget delivery due at 2.00'. With that the doorbell rang, and as Arthur made his way into the hall, he stumbled over a pile of toilet rolls. He opened the door to find no one there, but a 16kg bag of self-raising flour deposited on the mat. With some difficulty he wrestled the bag into the hall, then returned to the living room to try and find some explanations on his laptop. He was taken aback to find it buried under a pile of papers that were obviously work related. Before moving them, he glanced at the top one. 'Ongoing virus-related issues with Chinese clotted cream contract', it read. 'Most Secret'. What was all this work stuff doing at home?

He entered 'coronavirus' into Google, and the first thing that came up was the conspiracy theory that the whole pandemic had been caused by the introduction of 5G technology. Now Arthur's laptop was quite ancient so far as computers go — it was at least five years old — and it took exception to the sudden leap from 10th June, 2017 to the 25th April, 2020. There had been worldwide panic back in 1999 that on the stroke of midnight of New Year's Eve that computers would fail, aircraft would drop out of the sky, sheep would abort and life as we then knew it would end, to the extent that companies selected some poor sod, generally the newest recruit, to be at their desk as midnight struck in case the worst happened (although quite what they were expected to actually do was generally left to their own discretion). But nothing happened, because even the primitive computers around at the turn of the millennium could handle a transition of one second.

But nearly three years was a big ask, and Arthur's computer responded by freezing. Arthur sighed. This had happened before, and he knew the only way to sort it was to let the battery run down to zero. He closed his computer and went back to his paper, only to find Mish had reappeared and was now occupying the whole chair. As he moved Mish over to an indignant squawk, he was relieved to see the date had reverted to June 10th, and the headline was what a mess Theresa May was in.

That afternoon Arthur went into the garden to tend to his beans, accompanied by a watchful Mish who wanted to make sure the spiritual integrity of the vegetable patch was not disturbed. Jill took the opportunity of Arthur's absence to go on Facebook, only to find her laptop had gone flat. Jill and Arthur frequently resorted to each other's computers, but when she opened up his she was thrilled to find herself confronted with a new conspiracy theory. Being back in its own comfort zone, the computer had unfrozen, but try as she might Jill could not copy the link to send to herself. So, she printed the whole thing out, tucked the script away well out of Arthur's sight, and shut down his computer.

IV
Croydon, Thursday June 15th 2017

The following Thursday Arthur was out for the evening at the monthly meeting of his beermat society, and Jill had the chance to settle down and really study her printout. The main thrust of the paper was that the new 5G technology had been deliberately engineered to transmit bacteria and viruses, particularly the Covid-19 coronavirus, which in turn had been developed in Wuhan in China specifically for this purpose. Bats were involved somehow. Jill was no electronics engineer nor virologist, and at first sight it all sounded terribly convincing to her, especially as she'd never heard of either 5G or coronavirus.

The pleasure that Jill derived from her conspiracy theories was twofold. First, she found them an enjoyable antidote to the evasions and outright lies put out by official bodies such as the government and big business, and she found some of the ideas both intriguing and plausible. Secondly, she relished the social approval she gained by reposting the material online. Did she really believe in the misinformation she helped spread? Upon reflection, probably not. She would have been horrified at some of the dark forces behind these theories, and the potential for damage they could cause. But that Thursday evening all she could think of was that she was in possession of an electrifying new hypothesis, and she couldn't wait to post it. As it was in hard copy, she had to scan it in first, and so it was that the world first heard about Covid-19 and its links to 5G technology on Thursday, 15th June, 2017.

By the end of the evening, she had received thirteen likes.

V
Ministry of Peace, Beijing, July 2017

The Minister gazed with a mixture of anger and anxiety at his laptop screen. He was so upset he'd foregone his start of the morning game of Candy Crush Saga, which he found as inspiring and rejuvenating as his first cup of green tea. The call had come before he'd even left home that morning. A crisis had broken and he was the man to fix it. But he'd been left with the distinct impression it was because he had nothing better to do.

There was a knock at his door, and the Deputy Chief Scientist, Pi Kin Duk, was ushered in.

"One bow's enough," said Chen irritably. "Just sit down." He thrust the laptop at Pi. "What's all this? Why don't I know about it?"

Pi gazed with growing horror at the screen, before stuttering, "I don't know anything about this."

"What is the point of you, then?" demanded Chen, angrily. "Find me someone who does know about this — Covid-19, this coronavirus. And what our 5G has got to do with it." For the two men were looking at Jill's conspiracy theory, which had gone viral, and had just reached the centre of power in Beijing. Luckily, at least for the Chinese politburo, thanks to China's blockade of foreign websites, Chen and Pi were amongst the very few people in China who'd seen it.

"B… B… but it's nonsense," said Pi. "You can't transmit

bacteria and viruses by electromagnetic waves. It's impossible."

"Don't try and fob me off with facts," shrieked Chen. "I'm not interested in facts. I'm interested in opinions. And the whole world now thinks that our 5G system is going to give them a terminal disease! And furthermore, someone out there has got this Covid thing — and it's not us."

"What do you want me to do," asked Pi, weakly.

"Find this sodding Covid. And now fuck off."

As Pi slunk out Chen jabbed at the buttons on his phone, and bellowed, "Get me the Head of External Intelligence."

The following morning found Pi in the Director's office at the Wuhan Institute of Microbiology.

"What do you know about coronavirus?" he asked the Director, Hua Wei Pong.

"How long have you got?" replied Hua, a fresh-faced young man in oversized glasses.

Pi took exception to the implied facetiousness of the reply. "You're the one who'll be working to a career defining deadline," he snarled.

Hua was shaken by his reply. "Well, coronavirus is a pretty big group of RNA viruses that cause a variety of diseases in birds, mammals, and, of course, man. Outcomes in man range from the common cold to killers like SARS. What else do you need to know?"

"What about Covid-19? What's that?"

Hua looked blank. "I've never heard of that one."

"The world currently thinks it was isolated and developed by your lab, released via a bat into the Wuhan Wet Market, and disseminated globally by our 5G systems."

"But that's ridiculous," said Hue.

Pi finally found a smidgeon of fellow feeling for the young scientist. "I know it's ridiculous. But this Covid — thing — seems to be out there somewhere, and Beijing wants us to have it. They're not scientists," he added, gently.

"OK," said Hua. "I like a challenge. If they say it's bats, we'll start with bats."

VI
MI7, Silicon Roundabout, London, July 2017

The newly appointed head of MI7, Robin Parkington Smythe, gazed disconsolately around his shabby new office located just off Old Street. He supposed it just about qualified as Silicon Roundabout, and enabled the government to claim its cyber security services were at the heart of the most exciting techie hub in Europe, but if this dump of a premises was the best the government could come up with to house its widely trailed Cyber Security and Counter Conspiracy agency, aka MI7, things were grimmer than he thought. It was his first proper day in the job, and he had to start interviewing and appointing staff. On top of that he'd received an urgent request from No 10 to investigate some conspiracy theory that had just surfaced about an unheard of, yet deadly, virus and 5G.

He sighed and looked at his schedule for the day. First up was an interview with an allegedly brilliant young IT analyst in — he looked at his watch — Oh God! five minutes. He rummaged around the papers on his desk and looked at the young man's CV with growing dismay. He was only sixteen, had no formal qualifications, and had just avoided an extradition attempt by the USA for hacking the venereal disease records of the entire US military. But he was one of the weirdos and misfits currently favoured by elements influencing the government to 'put a rocket up the arse' of the established public service, so he'd better take it seriously.

Robin wondered if they'd even speak the same language.

There was a knock on the door and his secretary, a pleasant looking grey haired woman called Muriel, poked her head round.

"Number one's here, sir, Justin Bit."

A shifty looking youth looking considerably younger than his sixteen years was ushered into the office. He sat awkwardly in the chair across the desk from Robin.

"Hello, Justin," said Robin. "Would you like to tell me about yourself?"

"Wasn't my fault," replied the youth. "I thought we was just playing a game."

"But didn't you try and extort a million bitcoins from the US government?" asked Robin.

"That was the others."

Robin was aware the UK government had only narrowly been able to persuade the furious American security services of Justin's innocence. His next question, where Justin saw himself in five years' time, was pre-empted by his secretary.

"Foreign Office on the phone, sir. They want confirmation that Justin has been appointed and that you've tracked down the source of the conspiracy theory."

Robin bowed to the inevitable.

"Welcome to the team, Justin," he said. "I've got a job for you."

VII
Croydon, 5th July, 2017

It was a Wednesday evening, and Arthur and Jill were sitting in their living room. The One Show had finished, there was nothing on till nine o'clock, and Arthur was reading Jill's Guardian, which was revelling in the discomfitures of Mrs. May's government. Jill had her laptop open, surreptitiously looking at her conspiracy post, Mash curled up by her side. One hundred and three likes and forty-one shares! She gave a little wriggle of pleasure.

The doorbell rang.

"Your turn," said Jill.

"I did it last," protested Arthur. "The man who wanted to do our drive."

"Oh, go on. I've got the cat."

"It might be the Jehovah's Witnesses again."

"I thought they were Mormons. You made friends with them!"

"Oh, all right," moaned Arthur. "But you do the next two."

A minute or two elapsed, then Jill heard Arthur call from the front door.

"Jill! Did you enter a competition with… sorry, what's the name? The Jasmine Tree Chinese restaurant in the High Street? You didn't? No, I didn't. Oh! Hold on. Apparently, they picked us at random from the phone book. We've won a Ming Emperor meal for two."

Moments later Arthur returned to the living room followed by two Chinese men carrying a carrier bag of what was presumably their prize. Jill was a little taken aback by their appearance. They were very bulky, and dressed like extras from Reservoir Dogs. Nevertheless, they were very polite, obediently deposited the carrier bag in the kitchen, and left.

Jill warmed some plates, and opened up the foil containers. It certainly didn't look like something that would overjoy a Ming Emperor, but as she'd now stuck the shepherd's pie they were going to have in the freezer, they tucked in. An hour later they were both fast asleep on the sofa, and Mash, who'd helped himself to a couple of prawns, with them.

They woke up on an old mattress in a dark storeroom smelling of soy sauce sometime in the small hours. As they shuffled around trying to make sense of where they were and what had happened to them, a light was switched on, and they recognised one of the men from the Chinese restaurant watching over them. With a shock they saw he was carrying a gun.

"They're awake," the man called, softly, and two more men appeared, one the other from the restaurant.

"Where are we?" croaked Arthur. "Who are you?"

"Best you don't know," said the new man, whose name was Jing An Ling, and who seemed to be the other men's boss. The men were, in fact, operatives of China's Ministry of External Intelligence. The Jasmine Tree was the front for the Ministry in the UK. That was why the food wasn't very good.

"We would like to talk to you about this." He produced Jill's laptop, and deftly opened it.

"How did you know the password?" said Jill, indignantly.

"It wouldn't be 'password' by any chance?" said Jing. Jill looked suitably chastened. Jing presented them both with Jill's Facebook conspiracy post.

"Where did you get this?" Arthur was looking totally blank, but Jill shuffled uncomfortably on the mattress.

"Er, I found it on Arthur's — my husband's — computer." Arthur had no memory at all of opening that page during his brief trip to 2020. He shrugged helplessly. What a nightmare! Here he was, obviously in deep trouble, and not even on one of his travels.

"You must tell us," said Jing, in an increasingly threatening manner.

It was here that there was a further highly improbable twist in the story. For the Jasmine Tree was next door to the Jewel of Bengal, and if the Chinese restaurant was a front for the Chinese Ministry of External Intelligence, the Jewel was a front for the Indian equivalent (although the food was better). Their adjacent locations were no accident: they had been chosen by their respective agencies to keep an eye on each other, as well as on the UK. The Jewel had in fact some time ago installed a bug in the Jasmine Tree's storeroom, and were listening with increasing interest to what was going on.

Now the Indian agency had a very good relationship with the UK's security services, and knew the British were also under orders to find the source of this 5G conspiracy theory. A swift exchange of messages, and the newly established MI7 requested that Arthur and Jill be extracted from Chinese clutches. The Indians burst in, the Chinese were caught by surprise, and the following morning found Arthur and Jill sat in the MI7 building on Silicon Roundabout.

A couple of days later a report was duly passed on to the

Foreign Office. The male, Arthur Smith, had travelled forwards in time to 2020, had picked up this theory in the aftermath of a massive viral pandemic which had killed tens of thousands in the UK alone, and it had remained on his computer where his wife had found it and posted it on Facebook.

The Foreign Office wondered if MI7 had gone native.

VIII
MI7, Silicon Roundabout, London, July 2017

Justin had made, on the whole, a good start in his job. But being a 'weirdo and a misfit', MI7 had to take the rough with the smooth. The smooth was definitely his achievement in tracking down the source of the 5G conspiracy theory to an IP address in Croydon. But had he been a touch more security conscious, he wouldn't have then informed his worldwide gaming contacts of his new role in MI7 and details of how he'd cracked his first mission in no time at all. His Chinese contact who went under the username of Su Zi Wong was in fact a burly male employee of the Ministry of External Intelligence, and he had promptly informed his bosses not only of the existence of a new arm of the British Secret Service, MI7, but also of the origin of the allegations about 5G and viruses that had been panicking the top brass. The fact that the Chinese operation to kidnap Arthur and Jill had totally gone tits up did not diminish the value the Chinese placed on the source of the information in the first place.

VIII
Ministry of Peace, Beijing, Autumn 2019

"We have good news and bad news, Comrade Minister," said Pi Kin Duk, apprehensively.

"Go on," said Chen, grimly.

"Well, the good news is we have finally apprehended the renegades who absconded after their failed mission in the UK, Jing An Ling and his associates, and they are now in solitary confinement in a re-education centre in Inner Mongolia."

"And where did you find them?"

"They had gone to ground in Soho. They can cook quite well now. And we do now have a mole at the centre of MI7."

"And the bad news?"

"There's even more, good news, Comrade."

"Go on."

"We have isolated the Covid-19 virus in the Wuhan Institute of Microbiology. It was indeed found in bats."

"And the bad news?"

Pi nervously cleared his throat. "Er, it seems that despite our best efforts to suppress it, the conspiracy theory that bats were implicated in some kind of illness got out and there was a panic that they would be banned from sale. There was a surge in demand, and some unscrupulous traders starting selling bats — at hugely inflated prices — from some very dodgy sources. It seems like there's been a tiny outbreak of illness, nothing more than a cold really, in Wuhan."

"What was the address of that re-education centre in Mongolia you were talking about?"

IX
MI7, Silicon Roundabout, February, 2020

Justin's career had flourished in MI7. Whilst it was recognised that security was not one hundred percent watertight, that was vastly outweighed by the information gained from Justin's worldwide network of gamers. His capability and achievements were so highly regarded in the right quarters that when Boris Johnson was returned with a thumping majority in December of 2019, one of the first actions of Downing Street was to remove the incumbent head of the service, Robin Parkington Smythe, and replace him with Justin. Indeed, there were suggestions that MI5 and MI6 might be amalgamated into MI7 under Justin's leadership. That may well have happened had the Americans not objected to the fact that someone they were still highly suspicious of would have access to shared intelligence, and threatened to withdraw the facility if the plan was not scrapped forthwith. It was regarded as diplomatic to keep them happy, knowing that Justin's American contacts could hack the Pentagon at will.

Justin was at a critical stage in a thrilling new game with his Chinese contact Su Zi Wong involving playing God with the fate of galaxies — access to a new level depended on it — when an e-mail pinged into his inbox. 'Urgent!' it read. 'What the fuck's going on in Wuhan?'. He reread the message, and thought what a stroke of luck he had China on hold. 'Hi, Su', he messaged. 'Got a mo?'. 'Yo', was the reply. 'What's with

Wuhan?'. There was a brief pause, then, 'There's been an outbreak of something called coronavirus. Couple of thousand dead, complete lockdown, rumours of police shooting people on sight. And according to the WHO, going worldwide'. 'OK, thanx', responded Justin.

Justin replied with the information, and almost immediately received the reply. 'What the fuck do we do?'. Now Justin not only had national contacts, he also knew people within supranational bodies like the WHO, although he did find they were a bit more serious minded than his usual chums. Nevertheless, he got an almost instantaneous reply to his query, and promptly relayed it on. 'WHO says immediate quarantine of borders, urgent introduction of track and trace, cancellation of mass sporting events, complete lockdowns on a national basis'.

About half an hour later there was another ping in his inbox. 'You do realise that Cheltenham's coming up next month?'.

Newport Pagnell Revisited

I
Croydon, 6th – 7th July, 2017

When Arthur and Jill finally got home the morning after their ordeal, they found Mash had been sick on the carpet and was crossly alleging neglect and cat abuse. They went to bed in separate rooms for the afternoon, partly because they were angry with each other, and partly because they didn't really know what to say. Arthur's time travelling was now laid bare, but it was Jill's obsession with conspiracy theories that had landed them — and ultimately the rest of the world — in their predicament. The silence persisted through dinnertime, and even by bedtime they hadn't exchanged a word.

Arthur and Jill rarely had rows, and when they did it was more of the niggle and sulk variety rather than the Armageddon that some people enjoy. The sulks would persist till one or the other got bored of only having the cats to talk to, and Mish and Mash maintained a strict neutrality throughout. But the following day, after a silent breakfast, Jill said,

"We have to talk."

It was the moment that Arthur had been dreading but knew was inevitable.

"Aarumph," he replied.

"You have to tell me what's been going on," said Jill, correctly interpreting his response as assent. She had retrieved the list she had started. "Who's Edith, for a start, and Chad? And what was so important about sandals and nuns? And who on earth is — or was — Shemyaza?"

So Arthur told her. He didn't go into unnecessary detail on Edith, which made Jill even more suspicious. He related his adventures in Heaven, leading Jill to observe she might have been happier with her children appearing as buds rather than going through the whole rigamarole of sex, which Arthur hoped she didn't really mean. When he reached his role in the success of the American moon-shot, Jill insisted on googling the reaction of the NASA control centre at the news of the landing, and her eyes widened in in disbelief.

"My God," she exclaimed. "There you are!"

He was careful to tell her about the fallback position of faking the whole thing in a Hollywood studio, rightly believing she would be pleased in having that conspiracy theory part validated. She wasn't so pleased about his contribution to the introduction of syphilis to Europe, though.

"Is everything you did about sex?" she asked, disdainfully.

"No!" he protested. "And it wasn't my fault I was dumped in these situations. I went on to save the world."

"You sound like Gordon Brown," she sniffed. "Go on."

But she was quite impressed when he told her about the Andromedans and the team building exercise in Dover Castle which had prevented the world from evaporating itself in 1962.

At the back of his mind was how he was going to deal with his revisit to the University of Newport Pagnell in the early eighties, but first he had to break Mish's role in proceedings to her.

"It got even weirder," he said. "I found myself in America, at the time of the revolution, with Mish."

Jill's eyes widened, but when she turned to Mish he just looked inscrutable. Then she said, "What revolution?"

Jill had a pretty loose grasp of history at the best of times, so Arthur chose not to expand on that one.

"And then, of course," he said, "My trip forwards. But you know all about that one."

"You're not going to blame Mish for that one?"

"No. Innocent of charge."

"And that's everything? Nothing else I need to know?"

Arthur was not a good liar, but he made a supreme effort on this occasion.

"Yes. That's it."

II
Croydon, 7th – 8th July, 2017

Jill felt uneasy. She didn't believe Arthur had told her the full story. He had been quite vocal in his sleep since the whole business began, and while words like 'Edith', 'nuns' and 'Shemyaza' had been explained by his accounts of his adventures, others hadn't. She was particularly worried about the words 'Cathy', 'Chris', and 'Flightpath' he'd mumbled one night, and she'd added them to her list. She'd retrieved her battered photo album from the bottom of the wardrobe again and gazed at the picture of her emerging from a nightclub with Chris, and dated May 1985. There was also the dream she'd had of she and Chris walking off into the sunset together. Now, while she could be accused of gullibility in relation to conspiracy theories, that didn't extend to viewing dreams as anything but involuntary night-time fantasies, certainly not prophesies or revelations of past events. Nevertheless, she felt that something odd was going on, or had gone on, that Arthur wasn't being entirely upfront about.

Arthur, for his part, was agonising over whether to tell Jill the whole story, that is, his part in ending her relationship with Chris. Given the unpredictability of events, he was pretty sure the truth would emerge eventually, and it might be better to be proactive rather than being caught on the hop at some later date. And after all, it was Chris that had been unfaithful, entirely off his own bat, and Jill had obviously regarded that as crossing a red line. He'd simply been the vector, and she may have found out from a myriad of other sources. He began to convince himself that he had been almost irrelevant to the outcome, conveniently setting to one side the fact he had deliberately manipulated events to secure that outcome. Jill would surely see it his way. And what might she do anyway if she didn't?

Arthur found out the following day. He'd decided to clear the air at the earliest opportunity, and Jill had simultaneously resolved to confront him with her suspicions. She was livid, oblivious to Arthur's increasingly panicky pleas that he had had nothing to do with Chris' actions, and had not deliberately dangled Cathy under his nose in order to lure him away from Jill. Arthur watched in horror as Jill rammed some clothes into a suitcase and stormed out of the house, slamming the door behind her.

"Uh oh," said Mish to Mash.

III
Brighton, 8th July, 2017

Jill turned up on her sister's doorstep in Brighton. Her sister, Sandra, was three years younger than her, and had recently emerged from a painful divorce. She had bought a modest two-bedroom flat comprising the top floor of a Victorian house in the Preston Park area of the town with her share of the settlement, and was really quite enjoying single life. She was now able to explore all the alternative lifestyles that Brighton had to offer, and had enthusiastically experimented with, amongst other things, veganism, trans-sexuality, lesbianism and dying her hair purple. As Jill rang on the doorbell of her flat a squat, powerfully built person with cropped black hair and lots of tattoos emerged, and wished her good morning.

Although initially surprised to see Jill, Sandra welcomed her into her flat and said, yes, she could stay as long as she liked. Sandra's divorce had awoken her to the defiminisation suffered by women in marriage (pardon? said Jill), and if Jill was ditching Arthur that was OK by her. Jill tried to explain she wasn't actually ditching Arthur; an issue had arisen and she needed time to think, but this was airily dismissed by Sandra. Once Jill had tasted what Brighton had to offer — by the way, did you see Lucy on your way in? — there'd be no going back. Blimey, thought Jill, that was a Lucy?

Jill knew that Sandra had never really taken to Arthur. She had met Chris once or twice, and was almost as devastated as

Jill when they broke up. Arthur, who would have suffered in comparison to almost anyone at first sight, was no substitute so far as Sandra was concerned, despite Jill's protests that Arthur had hidden depths (what, being a world authority on beermats? was Sandra's scornful response). Equally, Jill didn't really like Sandra's husband, a self-opinionated sales manager who viewed the Daily Mail in much the same light as the Israelites regarded Moses' tablets of stone when he descended from Mount Sinai. It came as no real surprise to Jill when the marriage ended. Their respective attitudes had driven a bit of a wedge between the sisters, and their relationship over the years had narrowed down to seeing each other at christenings, marriages and funerals, and the dutiful exchange of birthday and Christmas cards. Nevertheless, Sandra was genuinely pleased to see Jill, and wanted to do the best for her.

That best was to take her that evening to a club in the centre of Brighton, which was way outside Jill's comfort zone. She hadn't experienced the sweaty and ear shatteringly loud atmosphere of a club since The Flightpath in Milton Keynes, and to this was added the general uncertainty of adapting to this particular milieu. Sandra dragged her onto the tightly packed dancefloor, where she found herself wiggling with representatives of at least five different sexes, before beating a hasty retreat when a small, powerful, black clad figure she recognised as Lucy sidled up to her. I knew you'd enjoy yourself said Sandra when they got home.

"Do you want to talk?" asked Sandra the following morning over a breakfast of goji berries in camel's milk yogurt. Despite being mildly hung over and silently vowing never to go to a nightclub again, Jill was grateful for Sandra's hospitality and obvious desire to help out so far as possible.

She was also aware that Sandra's recently expanded horizons had included stuff that even Jill might have raised an eyebrow over a few days previously, which might make her more receptive to what she had to say. So, Jill told her the whole story, as Sandra's eyes widened in astonishment. When Jill finished, Sandra insisted they recover themselves with a warming cup of quinoa coffee (very sustainable and loaded with positive life forces, Sandra informed her).

After Jill had managed half the coffee, Sandra asked, "So what are you going to do?"

This was the question Jill had repeatedly asked herself after storming out on Arthur, and she didn't know.

IV
Newport Pagnell, 1st June, 1984

Arthur had been devasted by Jill's furious and abrupt departure, and that, combined with the fact that having Mish on his lap was now his only source of emotional comfort, sent him back to the Newport Pagnell of early June 1984. It was the first Friday of the month, and Arthur knew it was the day of Chris' fateful liaison with Cathy in The Flightpath night club in Milton Keynes. God, this is like Groundhog Day, he thought miserably to himself. He would once again have to take the decision about momentarily interfering in Jill's life to secure his future with her. But had that future now ended with her finding out what he had done? And how many more times would he be dumped back in this situation?

He felt he had no choice but to proceed as he had done before. If he didn't, it wasn't only his future as he knew it that would disappear. His children wouldn't be, Mish and Mash would be with someone else (as it happens, they couldn't have cared less), and the Croydon Beermat Society would probably collapse. And what would happen to the Chinese clotted cream contract?

The following morning, he was up and out by eight o'clock, remembering to allow twenty minutes to start the Imp. He arrived at the car, fumbled with the keys and let himself in. Having made himself comfortable, he turned the key in the ignition, anticipating the usual obliging cough as the starter motor attempted to persuade the engine to do something. Nothing. He extracted the key, and tried again. Still nothing. The battery, which up until now had performed well beyond the call of duty, had finally given up the ghost. Arthur broke into a cold sweat. He jumped out of the car to see if there was anyone around who could help, but eight o'clock on a Saturday morning was not a good time to be looking for intelligent life in a university car park. But twenty-five minutes later someone did appear, and gave Arthur a bump start. He roared out of the car park and ten minutes later swept into Jill's village.

He was too late. There was no bus, and there was no Jill. And in that bleak moment, the car's engine died for the second and last time, and with it, Arthur's hopes for his future.

V
Brighton, 9th July, 2017

"Let's go out for lunch," said Sandra. "There's a new vegan Icelandic restaurant I haven't tried in The Lanes."

"I thought the Icelanders only eat stuff like whale and puffin," said Jill.

"They're attempting to atone for all the wildlife they've destroyed by going right to the bottom of the food chain. Their signature dish is plankton mornay."

Jill blanched. She hadn't yet quite got over the camel's milk yogurt and quinoa coffee (which had turned out to be slightly hallucinogenic). "Can we go to The Regency instead? My treat."

As they left the flat Sandra gestured at the large black car parked outside. "That monster yours?" she asked. As a great fan of Caroline Lucas, she eschewed private car ownership, especially gas guzzling brutes like Jill's Range Rover Sport.

"It is a bit big, I suppose," agreed Jill.

Jill was enjoying Sandra's company, but she did wish she'd shut up about Trump for a bit. The rest of the world had got over, or welcomed, according to taste, his shock election last November. As they were having their coffee Jill's phone rang.

"Hello, love," said Chris. "I'm so sorry. What time are you getting back?"

She was suddenly confused. She knew she was with her

sister in a restaurant in Brighton, but she had no idea why, or what, Chris was apologising for. She momentarily even wondered who this Chris was. "Can I call you back?" she said.

"Was that him?" asked Sandra. "I knew he'd want you back the moment you showed him you were serious. But he'll have learnt his lesson. If you're heading back, the traffic gets pretty heavy after five o'clock."

What on earth am I being serious about? thought Jill.

"Um, what with last night, and going to bed late," she said, carefully. "And the yogurt and the coffee, I'm not sure exactly what I have told you?"

"Well, that woman, of course, the one in his office," said Sandra, slightly huffily. "You know you can trust me."

On the drive back to Wokingham, Jill did her best to collect her thoughts, but try as she might she couldn't recall any bust up with Chris, or why she'd spent the night with her sister in Brighton.

Chris was effusive with his welcomes when she arrived home, but she was a little more cautious. He instructed her to sit down while he made her a cup of tea, and as she did, one of her cats, Mash, strode up to her loudly complaining that he had been starved in her absence, despite the counter evidence of several empty sachets of Whiskas. His brother, Mish, leapt on her lap and gave her a disconcertingly direct look.

VI
Croydon, Sunday 23rd October, 2016

Arthur was engaged in his favourite Sunday morning activity, moaning. His long-suffering wife, Cathy, gave up attempting to read The Sunday Times.

"I really don't know why you're being so miserable about your birthday, Arthur," she said. "It's not as if it's a big one. Anyway, they say fifty-four is the new thirty-four."

"I don't feel thirty-four. If anything, I feel bloody sixty-four. And I think I'm going bald."

"Well, if you didn't sit and stuff in that armchair all day… Come on, the kids said they'd treat you to a steak."

"First of all you accuse me of sitting and stuffing myself to death, then you invite me for unidentifiable animal and chips at that bloody awful place on the roundabout. I can't win!"

"I wish you wouldn't say 'bloody' so much. They did say if the steak house offended your fine dining sensibilities, we could go to the Jewel of Bengal instead. Apparently, it's under new ownership and they're trying a 'cuisine minceur'."

"Terrific. You pay more for less but still get the same old food poisoning."

"At least that would keep your weight down. I'll take that as a yes."

"I'll need to check my diary."

"What! When was the last time you went out in the evening? By yourself? Apart from your beermat activities?

And you count down the days to those."

"Do you know the most interesting thing about my birthday?"

"Arthur," said Cathy, patiently. "You tell me every year. And I'm rushing around trying to get everything together for this training course I'm on next week."

Cathy was a senior manager for one of the major supermarkets, and was attending a two-day seminar with an overnight stay on the implications for UK food law in the aftermath of the vote to leave the EU.

"Where is it you're going?"

"I've only told you twice. It's near Wokingham. I've done you a couple of dinners and put them in the freezer."

"I could have cooked," said Arthur.

"I'd prefer to come home and find you alive."

It wasn't a very long drive from Croydon to Bracknell, which is where the conference hotel actually was, but being a Monday morning, the traffic was slow on the M25, occasionally grinding to a complete stop. Cathy had allowed for this, so she was pretty relaxed and allowing her mind to drift, found herself mulling over her marriage to Arthur. They had met at university, and had had an on/off relationship during their three years there. After graduating they had gone their separate ways, but five years later, Cathy, with a failed marriage behind her, had bumped into each other on Waterloo Station. They went for a coffee, then a drink, and the old spark was reignited. They married a couple of years later, and Cathy joined Arthur in Croydon. Their marriage was not one to set the world ablaze, but Cathy was quite happy with that after the firestorm of her first. But she did occasionally yearn for a touch more excitement.

VII
Hilton Hotel, Bracknell, October 2016

Chris had arranged to meet a business associate, Thomas, for an early evening drink at The Bracknell Hilton. Thomas ran a small upmarket chain of estate agencies and was looking to sell, and Chris was interested. The meeting had been arranged for six o'clock, but Thomas was obviously running late. Bored with looking at his phone, Chris lapsed into a reverie, or more specifically, started thinking about his wife, Jill. He wondered if they were drifting apart. They'd been together since university, but despite their different backgrounds, his privileged and hers hand to mouth, they'd been a devoted pair. Things had begun to change in their early thirties when Chris had rediscovered his family's talent for, and enjoyment in, making money, which he sensed Jill found slightly distasteful. But it was last year's referendum on leaving the EU that had driven a wedge between them. Chris was a fervent Leaver, and regarded Nigel Farage as the early Christians did John the Baptist. Does that make Boris Johnson Jesus Christ then, asked Jill, an equally committed Remainer. The rift had extended into other areas of their domestic life, including the bedroom. Chris wondered if she was using the excuse of politics to distance herself from him.

Chris was jerked out of his thoughts by his phone. It was Thomas, full of apologies; he'd had a puncture and had no idea how to use the emergency tyre repair kit provided in lieu of a spare wheel, and could they reschedule? No worries, said Chris. He still had half his drink left, and was quite enjoying being by himself for once, so settled back into his chair.

Cathy had barely made it to the end of the day. She enjoyed her job, but not the requirement to have an understanding, if not a command, of food law, and she had found the day mind numbingly boring. It had not helped that the other members of the course, mainly men in grey suits, were apparently loving it. She had been cornered at lunchtime by one chap who was obviously enchanted at the prospect of replacing EU horizontal and vertical directives by a homegrown system, and dreaded meeting him again in the evening. She was in luck, though. The men in grey suits vastly preferred swotting over their notes in their rooms, and when she went down to the bar for a reviving gin and tonic, there was nobody there she recognised.

Chris was about to leave when he spotted an attractive dark-haired woman enter the bar. He paused as he watched her order a drink, and then, as she turned to look for a free table, with a jolt recognised her as Cathy from university. It was obvious she hadn't recognised him, as her gaze had swept in his direction in looking for a seat, before finding a table just behind his. Should he say hello? Although they'd been reasonably friendly through Jill, he hadn't seen her since their night together, and he didn't know whether she'd want to be reminded of that. He decided not to say anything, and gathered up his jacket to go. But as he shuffled past her table in the by now crowded bar, his trailing jacket caught her drink and sent it flying off the table.

"Oh! I'm so sorry!" he exclaimed. "I'll get you another one. G and T, was it?"

When he arrived back, fresh drink in hand, he was aware

she was looking closely at him.

"Good lord," she said. "It's Chris, isn't it? How are you?"

The last thing that Cathy thought about for the rest of the evening was food law.

VIII
Croydon, November 2016

Cathy had enjoyed her evening with Chris. There had certainly been a degree of flirtation, though probably no more than might be expected between two attractive people with a degree of shared history. Chris had bought her dinner and they'd split a bottle of wine, and then returned to the bar for a couple of nightcaps. They'd exchanged contact details, and said yes we must keep in touch, with all the likelihood that such aspirations generally have. When she got home, though, she didn't mention Chris to Arthur.

Chris also kept quiet about Cathy to Jill. He was quite confident she knew nothing of his and Cathy's second year tryst, but he still felt guilty about it. That was not the only reason, though. A few months back Jill had become suspicious of his relationship with an attractive young woman recently taken on by the business. Nothing had actually happened, but Chris recognised that some of his behaviour had, at the very least, been open to misinterpretation, and he didn't want to aggravate his relationship with his wife any further.

Arthur's behaviour was changing. It seemed to date from his birthday treat at the Jewel of Bengal and subsequent stomach upset. He'd derived a gloomy satisfaction from the fact that he'd been proved right about contracting food poisoning, but that seemed to precipitate a period of bad dreams and poor nights. Cathy was so fed up with being disturbed that she moved into the spare room. This went on for months, with Arthur becoming more and more distracted and self-absorbed. He refused to talk about it, and by the spring of the following year Cathy was definitely fed up. And then Cathy was sent on another training course.

VIII
Hilton Hotel, Bracknell, June 2017

The training course was in the same venue as the one on food law, but on the rather more interesting topic (apologies to those fascinated by food law) of coping strategies for supply given the Government's current hopeless confusion over the UK's post EU future. It again included an overnight stay.

On the way there Cathy agonised over whether to contact Chris. It had been over six months since they had met, and apart from wishing each other Happy Christmas there had been no other exchange of messages. She knew deep down any further contact was potentially dangerous, but by the time she was approaching Bracknell she had managed to convince herself that he was an old friend and it would be a shame to pass up the opportunity for a drink. So, she left him a brief voicemail message.

Chris' stomach gave a little lurch as he picked up the message. He had been thinking about Cathy rather more than he knew he should, and was equally aware that any further contact was hazardous. But he was thinking of organising a meeting for all his branch managers, and he could use the opportunity to investigate the facilities on offer at the Hilton, *and* ask Cathy her opinion. That's what any reasonable person would do! He texted her back, 7.00?

Of course, there was no mention of the suitability of the Hilton's training facilities, and at six thirty the following morning Chris sneaked out of the hotel hoping the receptionist hadn't recognised him.

IX
Croydon, 8th July, 2017

Up until his fifty-fourth birthday and the fateful meal at the Jewel of Bengal, Arthur's life had been pretty straightforward and, it must be said, uneventful. He had married a girl in his late twenties he had known from university, Cathy, they had had two children, and he had spent his career in the Civil Service. After his birthday, he had started having weird dreams about returning to the past, which had become more and more realistic, and more and more disturbing. But on Saturday, 8th July, 2017 he was returned from what was to be his final retrospective visit to Newport Pagnell, and his whole alternative, but lost, past and present was revealed. He was devastated, and spent the rest of the weekend in an almost catatonic state. Cathy departed for work on the Monday morning looking forward to a day of relative normality.

Cathy was feeling enormously guilty about her night with Chris. Shortly before his departure from the Hilton at six thirty in the morning they had agreed it would be best all round if they had no further contact, and that had indeed been the case since. But though Cathy was feeling bad, she had no intention of unburdening herself to Arthur as she'd done after the first indiscretion with Chris. Let sleeping dogs lie, she thought to herself. If only sleeping dogs would.

X
Hilton Hotel, Bracknell, 7th July, 2017

On the evening of his liaison with Cathy, Chris had sent Jill a text to the effect that the evening had gone on longer than he anticipated — when he'd got out to his car he'd discovered a puncture, he couldn't work the repair kit, nobody could come out till the morning, and unfortunately, he was stranded. Jill took the message at face value, but a couple of days later, casually glancing at Chris' car, saw no new tyre. This did arouse a flicker of suspicion. It had only been three or four months since the row over his attractive work colleague, and while Jill had forgiven, she had not forgotten.

A month later, Chris did in fact hold his branch managers' conference at the Hilton. While the day was strictly business, there were to be drinks and a meal in the evening to which partners were invited. Chris was standing with two or three colleagues and Jill at the bar, when they were joined by the agency's newest member of staff, a brash young man called Justin. Now Jill was standing with Chris' other two colleagues, and Justin had no reason to believe that she and Chris were married when he said,

"My favourite haunt, this, Chris. Saw you here a couple of weeks ago with your wife. Enjoy the food?"

Chris went pale and the following morning Jill stormed out of the house to stay with her sister in Brighton.

XI
Wokingham, 10th July, 2017

Jill was woken up on the Monday morning by Mash yelling to be let out of the kitchen. She'd slept in a separate bedroom, but when she returned with the tea, she took the tray into the main bedroom where Chris had remained, put it on the dresser, and sat on the bed. He sat up.

"You're going to have to get rid of her," she said. "I can't trust you to be in the same office."

Chris was momentarily thrown by this demand, then realised that Jill thought his Hilton assignations were with Alice, his recent recruit. He was in more of a dilemma than he thought. He'd hoped against hope that Jill would have been placated by his contrition, and wouldn't want to know identities. He decided it would be best to be honest, or at least almost.

"Er, it wasn't Alice," he mumbled.

It was Jill's turn to be stunned. "How many women have you got?" she asked. "Who was it?"

"It was Cathy," he said. "From university. We bumped into each other."

Jill went pale, as her mind went back to the day she'd had the row with Chris and been held up getting to him the next day. As she'd arrived at his flat, she thought she'd seen a familiar figure with dark hair hurrying away in the distance, and the flat itself had had a *smell*. But the reunion with Chris

257

had been so ecstatic these niggles had been driven from her mind, only to return full force now.

"It's the second time, isn't it? You did it at university too."

For the second time in a week Sandra found Jill on her doorstep.

XII
Brighton, w/b 10th July, 2017

On the Monday morning Arthur was still feeling so bad he rang in to work to say he was taking a week's leave. He moped around all day, and was no better when Cathy returned from work. She completely lost her patience with him, and even in the depths of his misery Arthur realised he was being pretty unfair to her. Overnight he decided to take another trip to Brighton where he could sit on the seafront and, between the screeches of the seagulls, attempt to clear his head.

The following morning found him back on his bench gazing at the pier. He was ruminatively munching on a salt and vinegar crisp when a middle-aged lady asked if he minded her sharing the bench. Not at all, he said, and turning to look at her while shuffling down the bench to make more room, his heart lurched. It was Jill.

Endgame

I
Dover Castle, July 2017

Captain B&Q had thought his thoughtful thoughts long and hard, until in fact what passed for his brain ached, and had come to a conclusion. Something had to be done. Arthur could not be allowed to continue to rearrange world history. It was not only the big stuff — reversing the result of the Battle of Hastings which had in the long run produced a massively aggressive and globally destructive Great Britain rather than the socially responsible Scandinavian nation which would have resulted from Harold's victory, or Arthur's role in introducing syphilis to Europe and coronavirus to the world. It was the little stuff as well. Arthur's chopping and changing over Jill had erased several dozen total strangers' family trees from existence.

It wasn't just Earth's future that B&Q worried about. It was his own. He was approaching his two hundred and fifty millionth birthday, which was the normal retirement age for an Andromedan, and to date his career had been one of sparkling success. He had been posted to Earth because he had been regarded as one of the safest pair of virtual hands in the Andromedan colonial administration. But Earth was turning into more of a challenge than even he felt he could cope with, not only because of man's deranged, murderous and wrecking behaviour, but also because of the sheer randomness of events occasioned by Arthur.

At the same time, he did not want to apply the ultimate sanction of uninstalling Arthur. He had grown quite fond of this odd little ape, and felt a debt of gratitude over the successful resolution of the Cuban affair, which in turn had done B&Q no harm at all in the eyes of his superiors. The Andromedan had learnt a lot about man during his tenure so far on Earth. Philosophically (B&Q was being extremely generous in applying this term to man), irrespective of nation, man was fairly evenly divided into right wingers and left wingers. Right wingers supported a tiny minority of very rich and powerful people in doing exactly what they wanted, seemingly unaware that gave them no benefit at all. Left wingers, in the name of truth, justice and self-righteousness, wanted all the money and power that the very rich and powerful people had to be given to them. B&Q decided that Arthur was a left winger because he was not totally irrational, and that reinforced his view to try and do something for him.

There was an option that was available to him, and that was transportation. If he simply removed Arthur from Earth, that would eliminate one variable from the equation, and B&Q felt that in a slightly more predictable environment he could reimpose a degree of order and, hopefully, sanity.

Transportation it would be then.

II
Brighton, 11th July, 2017

Jill had had a disturbed night. Quite apart from the emotional stress caused by walking out on Chris for a second and, possibly, last, time, she had had a very detailed and troubling dream. She'd actually discovered Chris' infidelity with Cathy while they were at university, not thirty-odd years later, and had finished with him then. A few weeks later she'd met a chap called Arthur at a barn dance, and settled down with him. It must be said the remainder of the dream was not terrifically exciting, other than an incident when they'd been captured by the Chinese Secret Service and rescued by the staff of an Indian takeaway.

After breakfast she told Sandra she needed to go for a walk to think things through, and decided to go to the seafront. She started off near Hove, and by the time she was approaching the pier felt in need of a well-earned rest. She would have preferred a bench to herself, but the sun had brought out the strollers, and the nearest seat had one solitary middle-aged man in occupation, disconsolately munching a packet of crisps. She sat at the free end, and he obligingly shuffled to the other end. As she settled, she was aware from the corner of her eye he was looking at her. Oh God, she thought, please, please don't make an approach.

And then he said, "Jill?"

She turned to look at him in surprise. She had no idea who

he was — and yet... With a growing sense of bewilderment, she recognised him as the man — her husband — from last night's dream.

"Arthur?" she said.

It was Arthur's turn to be startled. How would she know him? In the alternate reality that had actually become the real reality, she had only ever met him once, and that was in the excruciatingly embarrassing circumstances of Cathy's house warming party, of which he knew she claimed to have no memory. But she was continuing to look at him with a mystified expression on her face, and he felt he owed her an explanation.

"Er...," he said.

"There's something weird going on," she replied. "I know you, I know everything about you, but I've never seen you before in my life."

"It's a very long story," he said.

Jill would normally never have dreamt of inviting a strange man home, but in this very peculiar instance Arthur wasn't a strange man. And Sandra, with her alternative view of the universe, could be of some help.

"Shall we go somewhere a bit more private?" she said.

III
Brighton, 11thJuly, 2017

Sandra was a bit taken aback when Jill turned up with a man in tow, especially one as unprepossessing as Arthur.

"Shouldn't you give it a bit more time, love?" she whispered as Jill showed Arthur into the tiny living room. Arthur, once again, was simply letting events wash over him.

"I know him," replied Jill.

"Do you think a couple of hours is enough?"

"No, I know him from before. Somehow."

Sandra's reservations were still not fully allayed (nothing new there then, thought Arthur miserably), but she offered to make some sandwiches and coffee for lunch (not quinoa? asked Jill, hopefully). She bustled into the kitchenette and emerged five minutes later with a plate of sourdough (homemade she said, proudly) and seaweed sandwiches.

"Tell me your long story," said Jill to Arthur. So Arthur did.

Captain B&Q, meanwhile, was making arrangements for the transportation. A berth had been reserved on the monthly transduction beam to Andromeda, and in the same way as an Andromedan could assume human (or indeed any other form) to make his contact feel at home, so the berths on the transport could be transformed into any kind of configuration and style to accommodate and comfort their guests. B&Q had chosen Buckingham Palace. He had also gained permission for a companion to accompany Arthur, for what could be an infinite exile. All that remained was for B&Q to collect Arthur, plus companion, and deliver them to the transport. Whilst the project was entirely logical from an Andromedan point of view, B&Q recognised that Arthur might take a little persuading, if not coercion. He resolved, therefore, to readopt human form to make Arthur as relaxed as possible, and Charlton Heston dressed as Moses was as good a form to take as any. He also recruited Dom to assist him, who was thrilled to be able to take on the form of Sofia Loren again. It simply remained to locate Arthur, and within a nanosecond he had been pinned down to a top floor flat in the Preston Park area of Brighton.

It was mid-afternoon, with Arthur still in full flow, when there was a knock on the door of Sandra's flat. She went to answer it, and Jill and Arthur heard a little shriek of terror. Sandra stumbled ashen faced back into the room, followed by Moses and Sofia Loren.

"Hello Arthur," said Moses. "You remember Dom?" gesturing towards Sofia Loren. Arthur went white as Sandra and Jill shrank back into their chairs.

"B&Q?" stuttered Arthur.

"The same," Moses replied, jovially. "You need to come with us."

The three humans sat immobilised. Ho hum, thought B&Q, I'll have to use a local transduction beam. But he had yet to decide on Arthur's companion. Andromedans, having spurned sex some hundreds of millions of years ago, had no concept of terrestrial love or bonding. B&Q's tenure on Earth, though, had taught him that man appeared to prefer permanent relationships with women, or at least it was women they tended to share a house with, and two possible candidates were sitting bang in front of him. He dismissed Sandra on the basis of her behaviour on the doorstep, and so it was that milliseconds later, Arthur found himself with Jill in Buckingham Palace.

III
Space, Summer 2017

Arthur and Jill wandered the nineteen State Rooms of Buckingham Palace in total bewilderment. B&Q had thought, probably quite rightly, that to try and explain to them that they were being transported two thousand five hundred and thirty-seven million light years to the Andromeda Galaxy would only complicate things, and there would be plenty of time en route to acquaint them with their new circumstances. In the meantime, they could enjoy their carefully engineered surroundings, which B&Q assumed would be the ultimate aspiration for any Brit (he was wrong in this instance; it was the Americans that would have loved it).

Of course, it was not going to take two thousand five hundred and thirty-seven million years to reach Andromeda. Their transport, Transduction Beam ZX82, was one of the fastest in the Andromedan fleet, and a transduction beam travelled faster than light by a factor of several squillion to one. In terrestrial terms that worked out at about a month, which is the length of a typical luxury cruise and the point at which most travellers are itching to get off the boat and away from their ghastly fellow passengers and the constant threat of norovirus, so reasonably manageable.

But none of this had been explained as yet to Arthur and Jill. They had reached the Throne Room which meant they were approaching their second lap of the palace, and so they took a throne each and looked at each other.

"Why did Moses and Sofia Loren turn up on Sandra's doorstep?" asked Jill. "And why are we here? And what have I got to do with all this? Are you and I married again?"

Arthur shrugged helplessly, but a little thrill ran through him at her last question. As he struggled to assemble some kind of coherent answer, there was a loud knock, and with a flourish a door was thrown open and a procession of footmen filed in.

"Teatime, sir," said the lead man. "One normally takes it in the White Drawing Room."

They felt a thinly veiled disapproval at their occupation of the thrones, so hurriedly shuffled off them and followed the line of footmen to the Drawing Room, where a lavish tea was laid out before them. This was actually quite welcome as neither had particularly relished Sandra's offering, even if the sourdough had been homemade. They were ushered to their seats, tea was poured and they each picked a dainty sandwich from the stand before them, but as Jill turned to thank them and take the opportunity to ask what on earth was going on, they vanished.

They enjoyed their tea, but were taken aback when the process was repeated a couple of hours later with dinner. The same procession of footmen marched in bearing a series of steaming dishes, this time with what appeared to be a sommelier to the rear. As the food was being laid out before them, the sommelier discretely appeared to Arthur's right.

"May I suggest the Chateau Lafitte '87, sir?"

Arthur, whose knowledge of wine had barely progressed beyond the warm Piesporter he had drunk at university, nodded apprehensively. Should he have at least checked what colour it was? But it was fine, though he thought he preferred the Tesco house red he'd had last week. At least the bottle wasn't covered in dust.

They could barely move after their meal, and when Arthur looked at his watch it was nearly ten o'clock.

"Bedtime," he said, automatically, then went a deep red.

But it was Jill's turn to go with the flow, and she certainly wasn't going to sleep by herself tonight.

IV
Space, Summer 2017

Dom had been nominated by B&Q to accompany the travellers, and at a suitable point in the journey explain what was happening to them. He had been keeping a careful eye on Arthur and Jill but in his Andromedan incarnation, so they had no idea whatsoever of his presence. After the fourth day Dom decided they had settled in sufficiently to be approached, or at least weren't constantly looking over their shoulders or jumping at the slightest noise. Before making his appearance, he had had to choose a new guise after B&Q had tactfully warned him that Sofia Loren might not go down too well a second time. Dom had taken an interest in British politics, and he was a particular admirer of Boris Johnson. He was impressed by a man who was ready to act the jester both at home and abroad, so different from the usual stuffy image associated with British politicians. No doubt the appearance of such a familiar figure would immediately soothe any lingering anxieties troubling Arthur and Jill, especially if he made them laugh as well.

The pair were sitting down to yet another fully loaded tea (Jill was already worrying about her weight) when a door opened and a familiar figure wobbled in. It was, so far as Arthur and Jill were concerned, Boris Johnson, wearing a boater hat and a red plastic nose, and with a large artificial flower in his buttonhole. They watched aghast as the figure lurched over to Arthur and, bending over, shoved the artificial flower into his face. There was a pause, and then a stream of water hit Arthur on the nose, followed by a shriek of manic laughter from the apparition. Jill burst into tears.

This was not the effect Dom had anticipated or intended. He had obviously overestimated their capacity for fun. He staged a rapid retreat to reappraise his approach, and after a quick visit to Wikipedia decided a figure of reassurance, not fun, was required. Five minutes later Arthur and Jill, who had by now calmed down a little, were confronted by Mother Theresa.

"My children," said Dom, soothingly, and making a sign of the cross. "We have to talk."

Once Dom had explained to them, primarily for Jill's benefit, he was in fact an Andromedan but had to assume human form (well, strictly speaking he could have assumed any form he wanted, and had toyed with the idea of a grand piano) in order to communicate with them, things started to move forward, at least from Dom's point of view. They were obviously a little taken aback that they were going into permanent exile on Andromeda, but once Jill's hysterical sobs had subsided and Arthur had recovered from a brief faint, Dom thought it had gone quite well.

V
The Andromeda Galaxy, Summer 2017

Andromeda, of course, is a galaxy, a bit bigger than our Milky Way (with whom it's scheduled to collide in four and a half billion years just to cheer everyone up), and with a diameter of around two hundred and twenty thousand light years. It consists of about a trillion stars, each with its own planetary system, and the Andromedans effectively occupied the whole lot. They all considered themselves Andromedans, and were governed by a central authority, but it must be said the northern Andromedans rather looked down on the southerners as a bit simple, and the westerners considered the eastern diet as, well, weird. Easterners thought the westerners too fond of junk.

It was Dom's job to select a suitable home for Arthur and Jill, and with something like ten trillion planets to choose from at first sight this seemed to be a straightforward job. But Dom was a perfectionist, and he wanted one *exactly* like Earth, and in the end only one fitted that bill.

The first intimation that Arthur and Jill had that they were nearing their destination was when Dom, who had maintained his persona of Mother Theresa, presented them with a sheaf of tastefully prepared brochures of potential future homes. Jill, who had long wanted to move from Croydon, was quite enthused by this aspect of their exile, and entered wholeheartedly into the exercise. Dom had let his imagination run riot, and some of the options on offer were The Garden of

Eden, with the pair as a kind of trans galactic Adam and Eve, a seventies retro ranch in Dallas, and a recreation of Croydon, complete with the Jewel of Bengal. They both dismissed the idea of The Garden of Eden; Jill still wasn't quite sure of her exact marital status, and was not going to wander round in a fig-leaf till that was confirmed. Arthur was attracted to the idea of having Croydon to himself, while Jill, who had been an avid viewer of Dallas as a teenager, leaned towards the ranch. It was Dom who came up with a compromise; they could have Croydon as their main residence and the Texas ranch as their holiday home. After all they did have an entire planet to themselves. Dom didn't mention that they would be subject to ongoing observation and evaluation by Andromedan scientists. Man had been blissfully unaware of the Andromedan presence on Earth, and this was no different really.

They arrived at their destination exactly a month after leaving. Having gone through a passport and customs process that they didn't understand at all they were delivered to their home in Croydon, or New Croydon as Arthur liked to think of it. As they opened the door they heard a familiar yowl from the kitchen, and Mash bounded up to them complaining he couldn't remember when he'd last been fed, *and* the toilet door was closed, followed by Mish with a very cryptic expression on his face.

VI
New Croydon, late 2017

They settled into their home in New Croydon very well, and for one week a month they went to the ranch in Dallas. Although the configuration of their new planet was exactly the same as that of Earth, they did not have to fly several thousand miles to reach Texas. Dom had set up a reserve on the outskirts of New Croydon which could be configured into anything that he or Arthur and Jill wanted, so to reach their ranch was perhaps a twenty-minute journey by car. If they wanted to go anywhere else for a change — Paris, Manchu Pichu or whale watching off New England, for instance, all they had to do was to give Dom a couple of minutes' heads-up, then hop in the car and minutes later they would be at their chosen destination. Hotels were created to reflect national characteristics, so they'd be ripped off in Italian ones, treated with contempt in French ones and get food poisoning in North African ones, which all helped to create an air of authenticity. Should they wish to include the travel experience in their vacations, a virtual airport would be created where they could sit in heavy traffic panicking about being late, queue for hours to get through security and then have their flight delayed for three hours.

Day to day life in New Croydon was undemanding but never boring. To make them feel completely at home Dom had given them their old jobs back, but instead of the nightmarish commute into London they just had to hop in their cars and drive to the reservation. Arthur now had his meetings of the Croydon Beermat Society on a weekly basis, and the virtual members of the society were much more fun than the originals, even occasionally visiting the Jewel of Bengal for a curry together. Jill joined the local LibDems, and spent many a happy evening moaning about Boris Johnson and Brexit with her fellow Guardianistas.

Jill's two lifetimes had sort of melded. Her current circumstances were so weird that having two separate, yet concurrent, life experiences seemed relatively normal. Mish and Mash helped in that they had figured in both her stories, though quite how they'd finished up with them in New Croydon was beyond her. She had accepted that she was now back in a marriage with Arthur, and one evening, after a couple of drinks down their local, had messaged Dom that they wanted to visit the Garden of Eden, and had wandered around in fig leaves for an hour or two. She didn't think of Chris at all.

But Arthur was worried about Cathy. Of course, he didn't know because Jill hadn't told him what had happened between Cathy and Chris, at least second time around. He wondered if there was some way of getting in touch with her. He needn't have concerned himself. Chris and Cathy were doing a perfectly adequate job of consoling each other back at home.

VII
New Croydon, late 2017

Trevor, of course, was entirely unaffected by recent events. As a seasoned traveller of the universe, it really didn't matter that Arthur was two thousand five hundred and thirty-seven million light years away from home. And so it was that one evening in front of a less than mesmerising One Show, with Arthur mithering to himself about Cathy, and Mish on his lap, he suddenly found himself transported back half a billion years and face to face with God in the cosmos.

"Hello," said God. "It's Arthur, isn't it?" God's memory worked forwards as well as backwards. "How are you?"

God was very glad to see a friendly face, indeed any face. The Holy Ghost, who was never much use at the best of times, had gone AWOL several hundred millennia ago, and he couldn't remember when he'd last seen Jesus. He was going through those difficult teenage years and had insisted on a lock for his room. God preferred not to speculate why.

Arthur was by now so used to weird things happening to him that he quite happily took this turn of events in his stride. He was flattered that God remembered him and didn't seem to be cross for his role in introducing sex to his Creation. Putting aside the wars and death and general misery caused by sex, from a biological point of view it had all worked rather well.

"Would you like some tea?" asked God. "You're not in a rush, are you?"

Tea appeared as if from nowhere. It was not as lavish as Arthur had become used to, and the unleavened bread was a bit chewy, but it was very welcome nonetheless. God was obviously in the mood for a chat. In fact, there were several things he wanted to bounce off another being, one of which was the creation of life. His ambition was to create life in his own image, which Arthur had some difficulty coming to terms with. He knew he was in the presence of God and was enjoying his company, but from a physical point of view God seemed a bit — well — nebulous. He was sort of grey and misty and swirled around, and sometimes seemed to disappear altogether. But God then produced a picture that looked exactly like Michelangelo's David, and Arthur realised that was how God saw himself.

The first attempt at creating life in the Galaxy Andromeda had not been a success, and instead of looking like David the lifeform had looked like an influenza virus, albeit the size of a medium potato. God had been so discouraged that he had been on the verge of giving up, but now Arthur had turned up if he had any ideas what might have gone wrong, God was willing to give it another go. Arthur was pleased to have a concrete problem to get to grips with now the marketing of clotted cream to China was ancient history, and readily engaged with the problem.

As daylight faded into dusk, Arthur and God wrestled with the challenge. More unleavened bread was produced, which led Arthur to ask God if he ever ate anything else. God replied not really, but could Arthur suggest anything, so Arthur recommended the jalfrezi from the Jewel of Bengal, which was his personal favourite, and God said, yes, he'd give it a go. Towards bedtime there was a breakthrough, when Arthur

277

asked God if he'd considered genetics when trying to create life.

"What's that?" asked God.

Arthur gave God a quick tutorial on how viruses had the simplest genetics of any organism (better not go into prions he thought), a simple strand of RNA...

"What's that?" asked God again.

...while David had one of the most complex, and that was probably the root of the problem.

"You just have to create a genome of forty-six chromosomes, and bingo!"

"How do I do that," asked God.

"You can do anything. You're God," replied Arthur encouragingly.

So God knitted his brows and concentrated hard, and lo and behold an animated David appeared. To Arthur's surprise and God's satisfaction he didn't have a willy though.

VIII
New Croydon, late 2017

Back on Earth, B&Q, who had been receiving regular updates from Dom, was appalled at hearing of Arthur's rendezvous with God. The whole Andromedan civilisation was under threat. But it wasn't only heavenly events that were concerning him. Jill had begun to experiment with leading a dual existence. One day when Arthur was out, she had asked Dom to recreate Wokingham. She had then set off in her Range Rover Sport (Arthur had settled for a Toyota Aygo) and headed off to find her old house. En route she had stopped off at a pub and had had three stiff gin and tonics (drink drive laws didn't apply in New Croydon; in fact, no laws applied there), and then had continued to her house. She had found Chris there, and didn't get home till the following morning. Thereafter, she visited Wokingham at least once a week on the pretext of attending her LibDem group (is there an election coming up, asked Arthur). Did she feel guilty? Not at all. She was just running two concurrent existences and (so far) it was great fun. She did draw the line at conjuring up Idris Elba though.

From B&Q's point of view, this was a ticking time bomb. The Andromedans hadn't abandoned sex without good cause, and B&Q was fully aware of the damage infidelity could cause, even if strictly speaking Jill was married to both Arthur and Chris. He doubted Arthur would see it that way, though.

B&Q was regretfully coming to the conclusion that Arthur

would have to be uninstalled after all, but he decided to try one last throw of the dice. The pair had been under close scrutiny since their arrival by the best scientists in the Andromedan Galaxy, and B&Q sent their chief a missive outlining his problems and asking if there was any solution. Easy-peasy was the reply. The humans' genome was actually so primitive they had been able to map the whole thing one evening and still have time to go down the pub. Rather than uninstalling Arthur in his entirety, they could simply and easily uninstall Trevor. Brill, said B&Q, go for it.

He first had the, not inconsiderable, task of disentangling Arthur's dealings with God, but luckily things had sorted themselves out. God had not given his David any means of reproduction, but the virus, recognising an opportunity, had mutated into the sort of size we would normally associate with a virus, i.e., somewhere between twenty to three hundred nanometres, and had infected David. From that point it was a relatively straightforward process evolving into an Andromedan.

Next, he had to organise their passage back to Earth. He pondered setting their transport up as their Croydon semi so that it would be a seamless transition from New Croydon to the real Croydon, but he dismissed that. They would have to accommodate to the reality of their former circumstances, and it was best they knew what was going on. Once again, Dom was the intermediary here.

When Dom explained to them that they were to be returned to Earth, they were both, on the whole, glad. They had enjoyed their break in New Croydon, but fantasy had its limitations. Arthur still had a couple of prickles in his bum from his evening dressed only in a fig leaf, and Jill was starting to feel a little uneasy at having two men on the go at the same time. They were allowed an input into their accommodation for their return journey, and chose their favourite Premier Travel Inn in Dover. They were due to return on Sunday, 23rd October, 2016.

There was an elephant in the room on the return journey, though, which took the edge off their enjoyment of the Dover Travel Inn and its associated Beefeater restaurant. Neither of them knew which reality they were returning to. For Arthur, it was a source of constant dread, but even for Jill there was an element of doubt about which way she'd jump, given the choice. Each was aware it preoccupied the other, but neither could bring themselves to bring it out into the open. Perhaps they realised it would have been pointless; whatever happened was entirely outside of their control.

IX
Croydon, Sunday, 23rd October, 2016

Arthur was engaged in his favourite Sunday morning activity
— moaning. His long-suffering wife gave up attempting to
read the paper.

"I really don't know why you're being so miserable about
your birthday, Arthur," she said. "It's not as if it's a big one.
Anyway, they say fifty-four is the new thirty-four."

"I don't feel thirty-four. If anything, I feel bloody sixty-
four. And I think I'm going bald."

"Well, if you didn't sit and stuff in that armchair all day...
Come on, the kids said they'd treat you to a steak."

"First of all, you accuse me of sitting and stuffing myself
to death, then you invite me for unidentifiable animal and
chips at that bloody awful place on the roundabout. I can't
win!"

"I wish you wouldn't say 'bloody' so much. They did say
if the steak house offended your fine dining sensibilities, we
could go to the Jewel of Bengal instead. Apparently, it's under
new ownership and they're trying a 'cuisine minceur'."

"Terrific. You pay more for less but still get the same old
food poisoning."

"At least that would keep your weight down. I'll take that
as a yes."

"I'll need to check my diary."

"What! When was the last time you went out in the

282

evening? By yourself? Apart from your beermat activities? And you count down the days to those."

"Do you know the most interesting thing about my birthday?"

"Arthur," said Jill, patiently. "You tell me every year."